Pinkbeard's Revenge

Greg Trine

Art by Frank W. Dormer

Houghton Mifflin Harcourt
Boston   New York

For Steve, the second-best fisherman I know—G.T.

To my hero, Christopher—F.D.

Text copyright © 2013 by Greg Trine
Illustrations copyright © 2013 by Frank W. Dormer

www.hmhco.com

The text of this book is set in Adobe Garamond.

The Library of Congress has cataloged the hardcover edition as follows:
Trine, Greg.
Pinkbeard's revenge / Greg Trine ; art by Frank W. Dormer.
p. cm.—(The adventures of Jo Schmo ; [4])
Summary: Fourth-grade superhero Jo Schmo and her sidekick Raymond face Dr.
Dastardly and Numbskull, who break out of jail and join forces with Pinkbeard's
band of time-traveling pirates in an evil revenge plot.
[1. Superheroes—Fiction. 2. Pirates—Fiction. 3. Time travel—Fiction. 4. Dogs—Fiction.
5. San Franciso (Calif.)—Fiction. 6. Humorous stories.] I. Dormer, Frank W., illustrator.
II. Title.
PZ7.T7356Pin 2013
[Fic]—dc23
2012046799

ISBN: 978-0-547-80797-3 hardcover
ISBN: 978-0-544-45601-3 paperback

Manufactured in the U.S.A.
DOC 10 9 8 7 6 5 4 3 2 1
4500519320

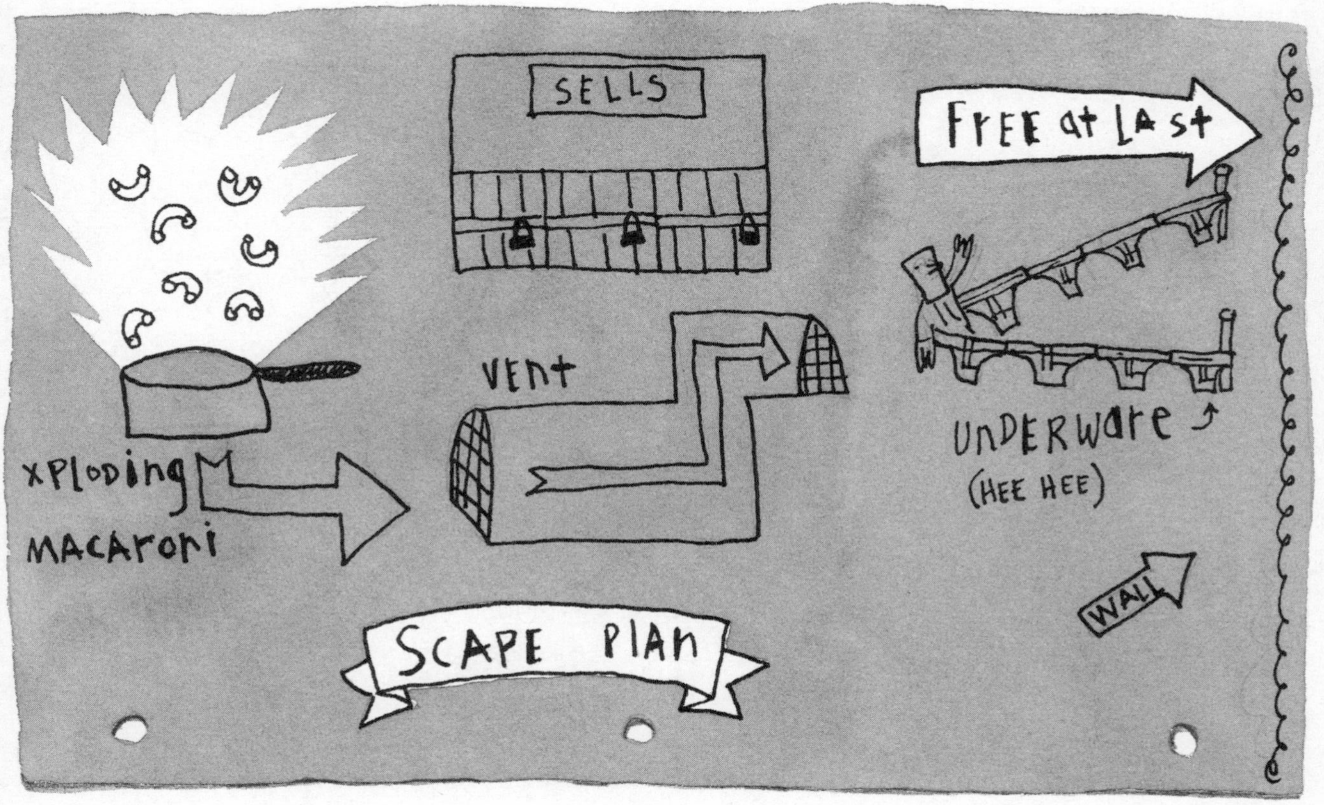
SELLS
FrEE at LAst
vent
xPloDing
MACAroni
UnDERware
(HEE HEE)
WALL
SCAPE PlAn

Contents

Slobber to the Rescue

Superhero Jo Schmo was speeding through the streets of San Francisco on her Schmomobile. Her dog, Raymond, sat in the sidecar, giving her a look that said, "Faster, Jo. Someone's trying to blow up the bridge."

The bridge in question was none other than the Golden Gate Bridge, and Raymond was right—someone *was* trying to blow it up. And this someone was Dyno-Mike's younger brother, Dyno-Harvey. You might be thinking that Dyno-Harvey sounds ridiculous. You're not alone. Dyno-Harvey would agree with you. But there was already a Dyno-Mike. What could he do?

Still, having a ridiculous name doesn't mean you can't be an effective bridge-blower-upper. Dyno-Harvey came from a long line of people who knew how to blow things up, and he had a truckload of dynamite. Any minute now he'd light the fuse and the bridge would be history.

But first things first. There were rules. Before you set off an explosion, you had to throw your head back and let out an evil laugh. Harvey also came from a long line of expert evil laughers. He stopped the truck in the middle of the bridge. Then he threw his head back and—

"Mwah-ha-ha!"

"Faster, Jo!" Raymond's look said. "I just heard an evil laugh."

Jo gunned the engine, and the Schmomobile picked up speed. Moments later she turned onto the bridge and saw Dyno-Harvey standing next to a truck full of dynamite with a match in his hand.

"*Mwah-ha-ha!*" Then he lit the dynamite.

"Faster!" Raymond's look said.

It was a long fuse, long enough for Dyno-Harvey to get away from the explosion. But Jo knew she wouldn't get there in time, not before the dynamite went off. There was only one thing to do. She grabbed Raymond by the collar and hurled him forward.

"Pork chops, Raymond. Pizza. Meatballs. Bacon."

Raymond flew through the air with his cape flapping behind him. The cape made him drool like crazy, and hearing Jo calling out his favorite foods made it even worse.

Or better.

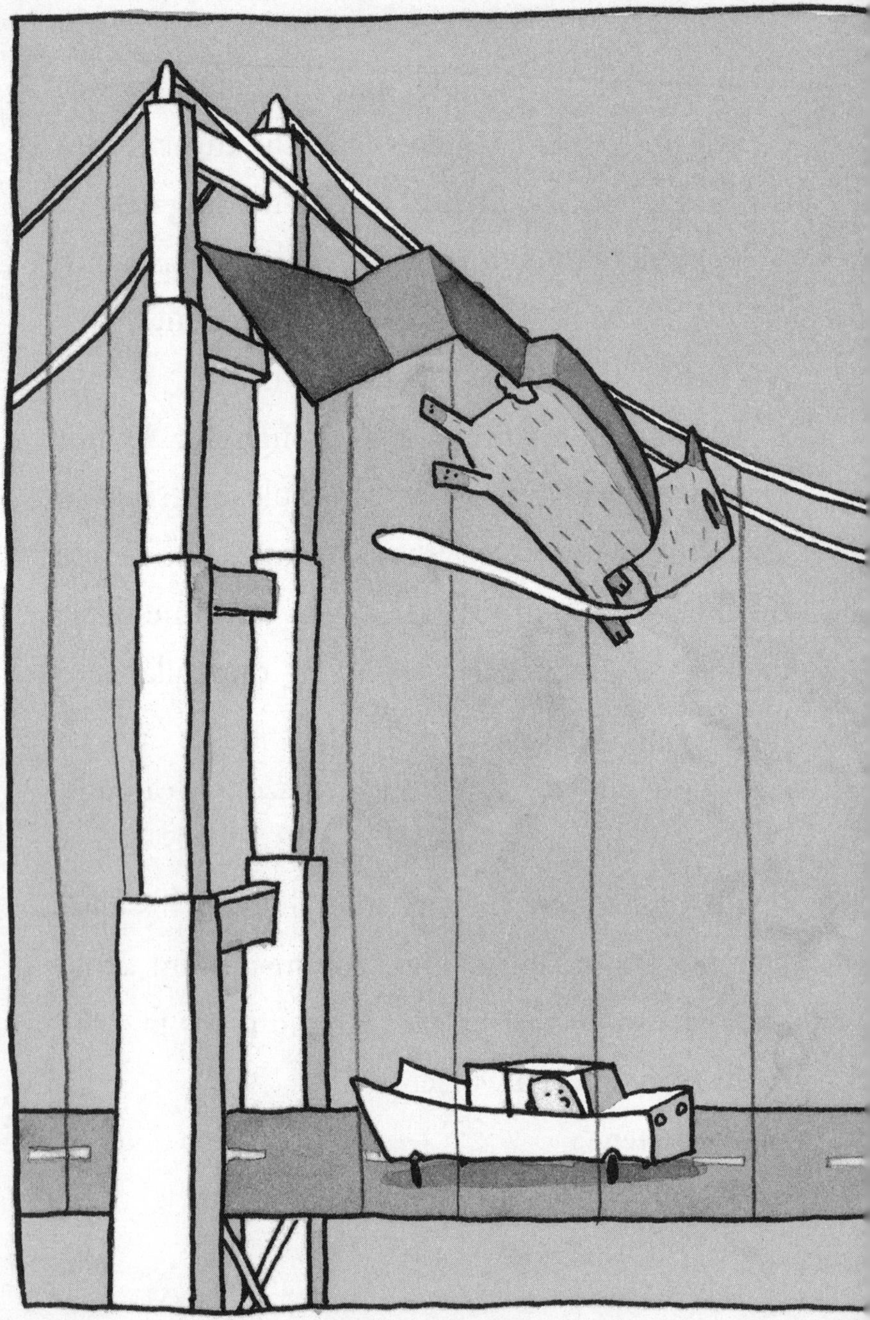

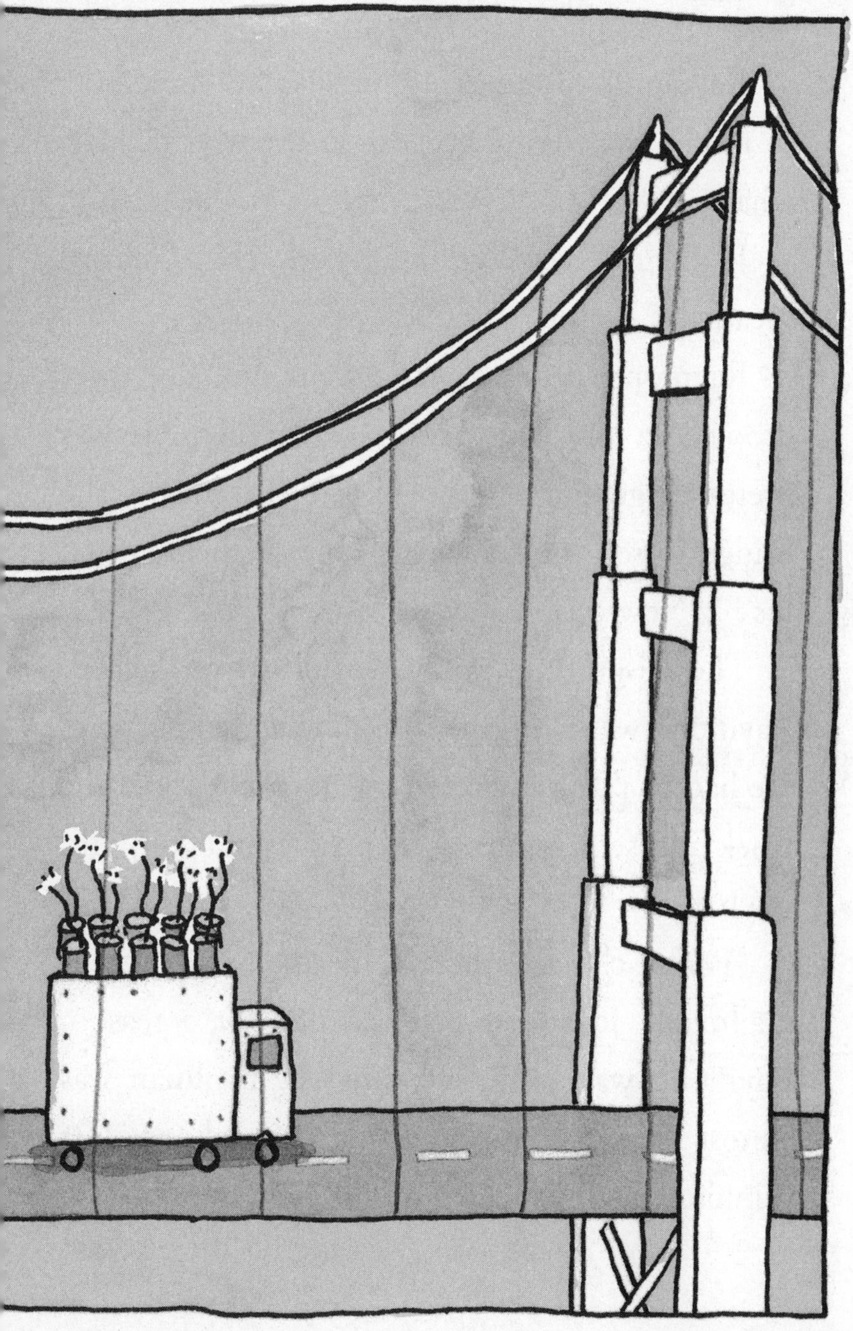

Raymond wasn't flying because he knew how to fly. He was flying because Jo threw him. Hey, whatever works.

Jo Schmo kept yelling. "Pork chops, pizza, meatballs, bacon."

Raymond drooled more than any dog ever drooled in the long history of drooling. It was pretty disgusting. Some of the drivers on the bridge tossed their cookies. One of them tossed his Fig Newtons.

The disgusting slobber couldn't be helped. Raymond was flying and drooling with a purpose. He had to put out that fuse before it reached the truck and sent hundreds of people plunging into the bay.

"Pork chops, pizza, meatballs, bacon— mailman." Jo added that last one for a reason. Raymond was a dog. Chasing the mailman was almost as much fun as eating pork chops. Just thinking about it made him drool even more.

And before you could say "The flying Raymond drooled all over the fuse and put it out," the flying Raymond drooled all over the fuse and put it out.

Seconds later, Jo Schmo pulled to a stop and high-fived her dog. "Great work, Raymond. You're the best drooling sidekick a superhero ever had."

All around them, people got out of their cars and cheered.

Raymond wagged his tail. "This is the best day ever," his look said.

Dr. Dastardly and Numb Skull

Only it wasn't the best day ever. It was a pretty rotten day. Jo and Raymond just didn't know it yet. Danger was lurking all over the place. That's the thing about danger: it lurks when you least expect it, like when you're saving people on a bridge.

Not far from San Francisco there was a prison, and in this prison sat Dr. Dastardly, otherwise known as the Bad Doctor. Or at least the dastardly one. Dr. Dastardly hated prison life. You would think a bad guy would like to be with other bad guys. Not Dr. Dastardly. He kind of missed his mom.

"Curse you, Jo Schmo," Dr. Dastardly said, waving a fist in the air.

Dr. Dastardly wasn't the only one who hated Jo Schmo. The prison was full of bad guys who had been captured by Jo and Raymond. One of them was Numb Skull, and he was sitting right across the table from Dr. Dastardly.

"You hate Jo Schmo?" Numb Skull asked.

"I do."

"And her little dog, too?"

"Absolutely. He drools way too much."

"I know," said Numb Skull. "More than any dog ever drooled."

"In the long history of drooling," added Dr. Dastardly.

"Exactly."

And right then, Dr. Dastardly stopped thinking about how much he missed his mom. For the first time since he had been sent to prison, he smiled. And what made him smile? The thought of getting back at Jo Schmo. "Revenge," Dr Dastardly said out loud.

"Revenge?" Numb Skull leaned forward. "Against Jo Schmo?"

He nodded.

"And her little dog, too?"

"And her little dog, too."

Numb Skull also had been missing his mom. But not anymore. He had a purpose now. He had a mission—to get back at Jo Schmo and her canine sidekick.

"I'm in," Numb Skull said. "What's the plan?"

"The plan is to break out of here and go after that little fourth grade superhero."

"Details, Bad Doctor?" Numb Skull wasn't the best planner in the world, mostly because his brain was a little . . . numb. Too many years spent in the boxing ring will do that to you. He'd leave the details of their escape to Dr. Dastardly.

Each day the two of them met in the prison cafeteria or out in the prison yard to discuss their escape plan. And their revenge-against-Jo-Schmo plan. But they had to be careful. The prison walls had ears.

So did the guards.

They also had eyes and noses, but let's not get ahead of ourselves.

The plan involved exploding macaroni and a giant slingshot big enough to launch a couple of bad guys over the prison wall.

"You must be joking," Numb Skull said when he heard it. "Exploding macaroni? That's the plan?"

"Don't forget the giant slingshot."

Numb Skull hadn't forgotten about the giant slingshot. He was just trying to ignore it. "Are you pulling my leg?"

"Trust me," Dr. Dastardly said. "I'm a doctor."

"A doctor with a dumb plan," Numb Skull said under his breath.

"I heard that," said the Bad Doctor.

The Tasmanian Chop

After saving the Golden Gate Bridge and all the people on it, some of whom were tossing their cookies from seeing Raymond drool like no dog ever drooled in the long history of drooling, Jo and her sidekick high-fived each other all the way home. Steering a speeding Schmomobile while high-fiving is not recommended, but if anyone could do it, Jo Schmo could.

And she did—quite effectively.

When she got home, she parked the

Schmomobile and went into the backyard to find her grandpa. Grandpa Joe, that is. It can be a little complicated having two Joes in one household—Jo and Joe.

Jo found Joe in his backyard shack.

"We did it, Gramps," Jo said, opening the door and going inside. "We saved the bridge."

"Great work, Jo."

"What's next?" Jo asked.

Grandpa Joe was a retired sheriff and an expert what's-nexter. He pointed to the police radio and said, "Not much going on, Jo. We wait."

Jo was *not* an expert waiter.

"Got any new moves to show me?" she asked.

"Moves?" Grandpa Joe asked.

"Fighting moves," Jo said. "Hand-to-hand combat stuff."

Jo had already perfected the Russian Toe Hold, not to mention the Siberian Ear Tweak. She was also the master of the Knuckle Sandwich. But those were yesterday's moves. Jo wanted something new.

"Have you ever heard of the Tasmanian Chop?" Grandpa Joe asked.

Jo shook her head. She'd heard of pork chops, but that wasn't exactly a move. "How does the Tasmanian Chop work?"

"Put your face over here and I'll show you."

Jo moved closer—

CHOP!

"Ouch!" Jo said. It was the second-best move she had ever seen—or felt. Not as good as the Knuckle Sandwich, but close.

"Okay, my turn, Gramps," Jo said. "Put your face over here."

Gramps leaned closer—

CHOP!

"Ouch!"

All afternoon Jo and Joe worked on the Tasmanian Chop, while Raymond watched.

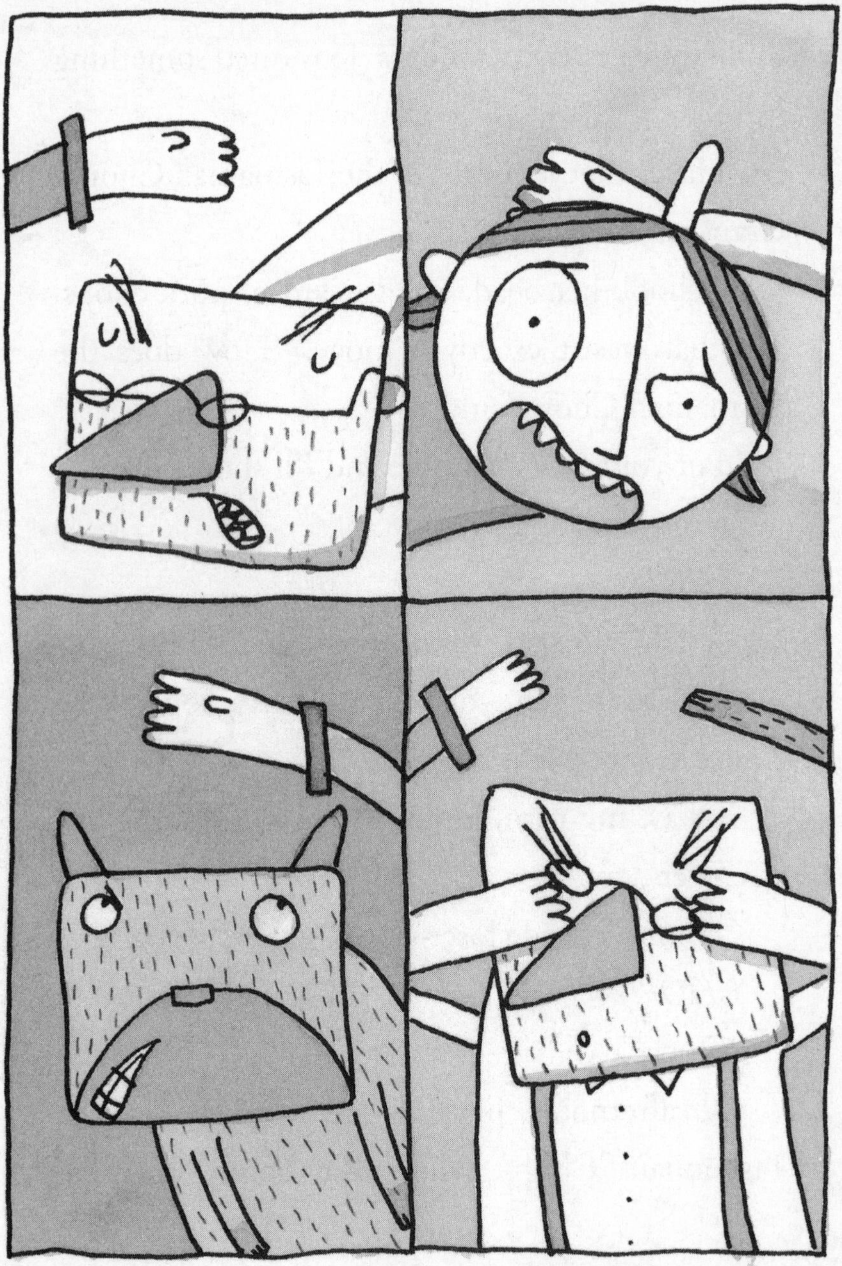

Raymond wasn't all that interested in the Tasmanian Chop. He preferred the pork variety. But what could he do? Sometimes you just had to watch boring combat moves.

And the reason for the boring combat moves was that Jo Schmo and her grandpa didn't think much was going on in the crime world.

They were wrong. Plenty was going on. While they were smacking each other with the Tasmanian Chop, Dr. Dastardly and Numb Skull were planning their prison break and plotting their revenge against Jo Schmo.

And her little dog, too.

Not only that, but time-traveling pirates were heading to San Francisco to rob and steal and do all sorts of other piratey things, like drink grog and chase women.

But more about that later.

Pinkbeard

On second thought, let's talk about it now.

The reason the pirates were traveling through time was that they were greedy. They'd already robbed and stolen and done all sorts of other piratey things—like drink grog and chase women—in their own time. But they wanted more. Much more.

Maybe people had more money to rob in the future. And maybe the grog tasted better and the women were cuter.

This is what Pinkbeard, the leader of the pirates, thought, anyway.

You might be thinking that Pinkbeard is a pretty ridiculous name for a pirate. You're not alone. Pinkbeard would agree with you. He used to call himself Blackbeard, but he'd drunk so much pink lemonade over the years that his beard had changed from black to pink. It happens. You can't exactly call yourself Blackbeard if your beard is the color of bubblegum.

Still, he was the leader of a band of pirates, which isn't too shabby for a guy with a pink beard. And these were not your average pirates. These guys were time travelers. *Greedy* time travelers. *Grog-loving* greedy time travelers. *Tattooed* grog-loving, greedy time travelers. Well, you get the idea. Pinkbeard was the leader of some . . . interesting fellows.

"Let's head to the future," Pinkbeard called out.

"How far?" asked Bart. Bart was second in

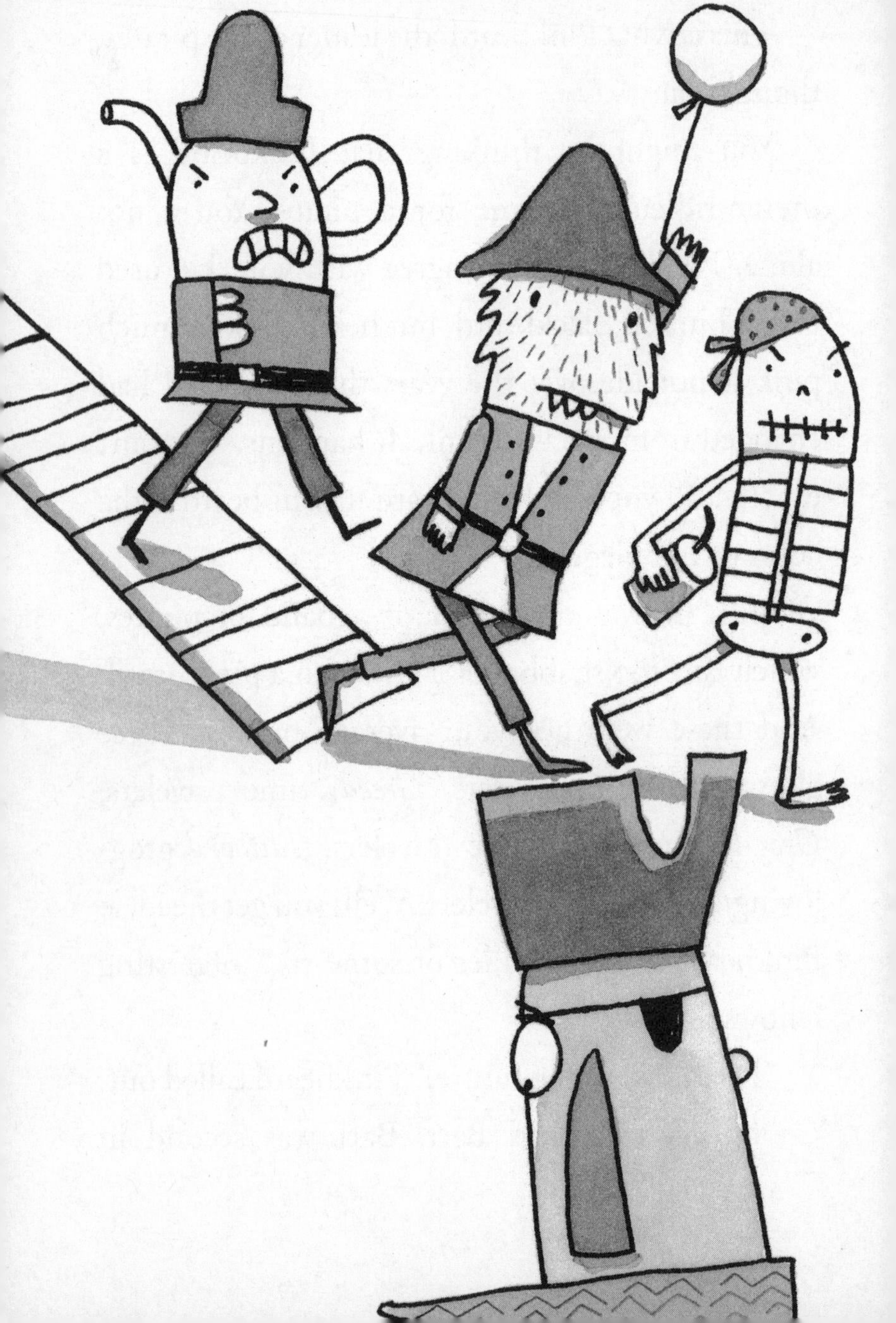

command and in charge of moving the pirate ship through time.

"Far," Pinkbeard grunted. "As far as possible." He just hoped they had good lemonade in the future.

Bart turned the dial, which was right next to the ship's wheel, all the way to 20—, which is code for sometime this century.

SPROINK!

You might be thinking that a time-traveling pirate ship would go *WHOOSH!* when it traveled through time. Not this pirate ship. Not one operated by a bunch of . . . interesting fellows.

Interesting fellows prefer more unique sound effects.

Anyway, Pinkbeard and his gang shot through time to the current century. Then they tied off to one of the piers and headed out to explore San Francisco.

"What's the plan, boss?" Bart asked.

"The plan is to do piratey things," Pinkbeard replied.

"Like rob and steal?" Bart asked.

"And drink grog and chase women."

But where to begin? San Francisco was a big place. Pinkbeard and his gang walked along the wharf, looking for ideas.

And suddenly, there it was. A flyer posted on a wall read:

Wine Tasting and Fashion Show
open to the public
especially if you're rich

"Ahoy!" said Pinkbeard. This was what you call a triple whammy. Everything they were after in one place. They could rob and steal . . . and drink grog and chase women.

"I love the future already," said Bart.

Too bad it's not Lemonade Tasting and Fashion Show, thought Pinkbeard.

Oh, well, at least they had rich people to rob and girls to chase. Two out of three isn't bad.

5

Dr. Dastardly's Evil Plan

Numb Skull still didn't like Dr. Dastardly's plan. Exploding macaroni? A giant slingshot? But he really did want to escape, because he really did miss his mom. More important, he wanted to get back at Jo Schmo and her slobbering sidekick for sending him to jail in the first place.

So he went along with the plan.

Since Numb Skull worked in the prison laundry, it was his job to steal the elastic waistbands from all the underwear. They would need lots of elastic to launch two bad guys over the prison wall.

Day after day he stole the elastic waistbands from the underwear, and soon the inmates began walking funny because their underwear was falling down inside their pants. If you ever see prison inmates walking funny because their underwear has fallen down inside their pants, you should point and laugh. They hate that.

Meanwhile, Dr. Dastardly, who worked in the prison kitchen, made progress on the exploding macaroni. Things were going so well that he almost let out an evil laugh. As you know, there are rules: Before you make a successful prison break, you have to throw your head back and let out an evil laugh. But if he did that, the guards would come running.

So no evil laugh—not yet.

Not until after the—

• • •

KABOOM!

"*Mwah-ha-ha!*"

It was the day of the prison break. A gigantic pot of macaroni had just exploded. This was followed by Dr. Dastardly's evil laugh. Macaroni flew in every direction—up, down, sideways, diagonally—you name it. The prison warden came running. So did the guards. And then—

KABOOM!

Another pot went off. This was Dr. Dastardly's plan. The pots were set to explode at different times. Just when the guards thought they were getting things under control—*KABOOM!*—more flying macaroni.

Dr. Dastardly ran outside for part two of his evil plan. He found Numb Skull on the prison football field, tying the underwear elastic to the goalpost.

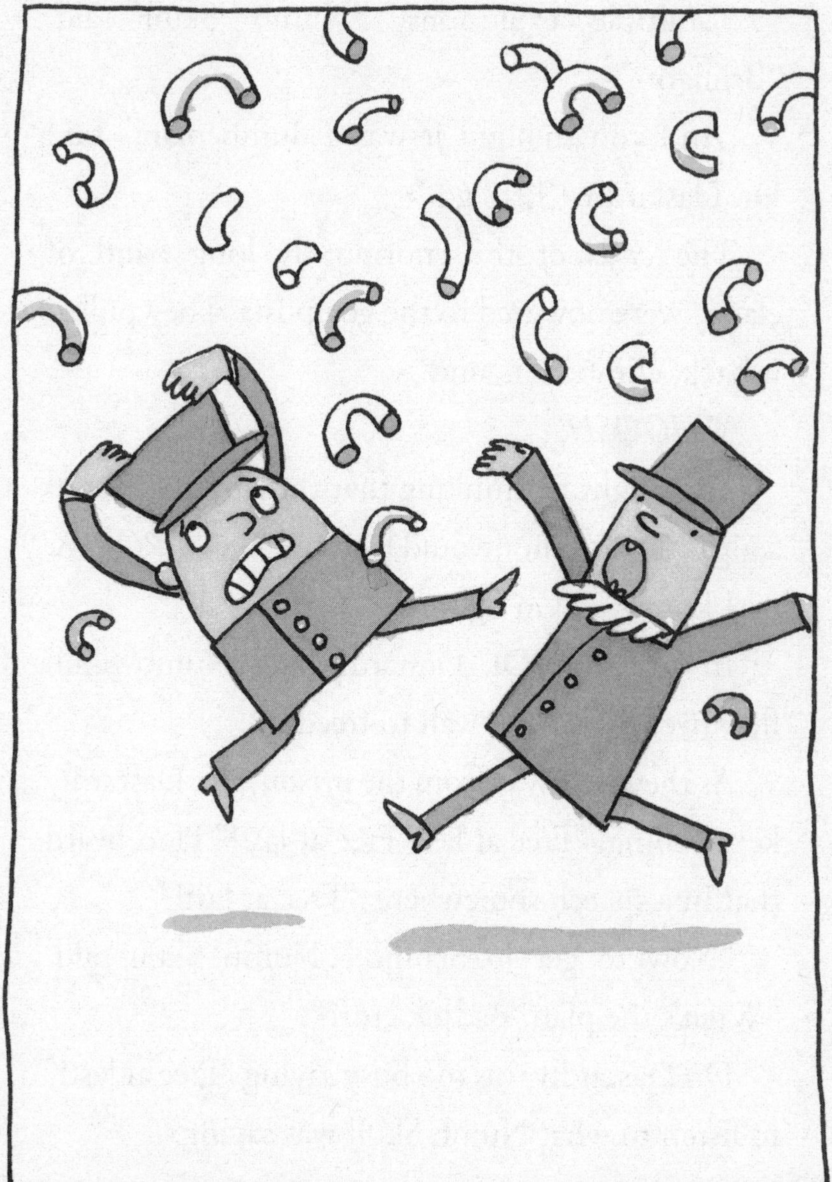

"Multiple explosions," Numb Skull said. "Brilliant."

"And you thought it was a dumb plan," said Dr. Dastardly. "Let's go."

The ends of the enormously long band of elastic were now tied to the goalposts. They pulled it back, climbed in, and—

WHOOSH!

You might be thinking that the sound effect of a gigantic slingshot would be more like *SPROINK!*

I know . . . Go figure.

In any case, Dr. Dastardly and Numb Skull flew over the prison wall to freedom.

As they ran away from the prison, Dr. Dastardly kept yelling, "Free at last! Free at last!" He'd heard that in a speech somewhere. "Free at last!"

"Now to get Jo Schmo," Numb Skull said. "What's the plan, Bad Doctor?"

Dr. Dastardly was too busy saying "Free at last!" to listen to what Numb Skull was saying.

"What's the plan?" Numb Skull yelled.

"Free at la—" Dr. Dastardly stopped. He turned to Numb Skull. "What?"

"The plan? The get-back-at-Jo-Schmo plan?"

"And her little dog, too?"

"Of course her little dog, too," said Numb Skull.

Dr. Dastardly grinned. "Follow me."

Poof!

Jo Schmo had no idea that Dr. Dastardly and Numb Skull were now on the loose, and that they were out to get her and Raymond. Nor did she know that time-traveling pirates were in town. She was too busy perfecting the Tasmanian Chop.

"Put your face over here, Raymond."

CHOP!

"Ouch!" Raymond's look said. "Can we stop now? I think you have it down."

Jo thought so too. *Time to work on other superhero skills,* she said to herself. "Break out the *Superhero Instruction Manual,* Gramps."

Grandpa Joe grabbed the manual from the bookshelf and flipped it open. "What's your pleasure, Jo?"

Jo wasn't sure. She made a list of the powers she already had:

Train stopping.

Flying.

Shape-shifting.

Various combat moves, like the Russian Toe Hold and the Tasmanian Chop.

"How about invisibility?" she said. Jo had once shape-shifted into a frog, jumped into her grandfather's shirt pocket, and gotten into the movies for free. But walking into the theater on her own because she was invisible sounded even better. Plus, invisibility would help her catch bad guys.

"Does it say anything about invisibility?" Jo asked again.

Grandpa Joe scanned the table of contents. Then he flipped to the appropriate chapter. "Hmm . . . It says that turning invisible is all about thinking invisible thoughts."

"Not again," Jo grumbled. This was one strange *Superhero Instruction Manual.* Flying was all about thinking lofty thoughts. Shape-shifting was all about thinking shape-shifting thoughts. And now this. "What's an invisible thought, Gramps?"

"Beats me. Thoughts that aren't there? Try thinking of nothing, Jo."

Jo tried, but it didn't work. Every time she tried to think of nothing, it felt like something. After all, a nonthought is still a thought. "This is impossible," she said. "There's no such thing as nonthinking."

"Keep trying," Grandpa Jo said.

All afternoon Jo kept at it. *Invisible thoughts,* she muttered to herself as she paced back and forth. *How can you think of something that's not there?* The only time she had ever seen anything vanish was when a magician came to her school. And it didn't really vanish. It was just a card trick. One second the card was there, and the next second—*poof!*—it was gone. Vanished. Invisible.

"That's it!" Jo said.

"What's it?" Grandpa Joe asked.

"Yeah, what's it?" Raymond's look said.

"We just need the right sound effects, Gramps. Watch this." Jo snapped her fingers and said, *"Poof!"*

She vanished into thin air.

At least she didn't say *"SPROINK."*

"Where'd you go, Jo?"

"I'm right here, Grandpa."

Grandpa Joe stared at the empty space where

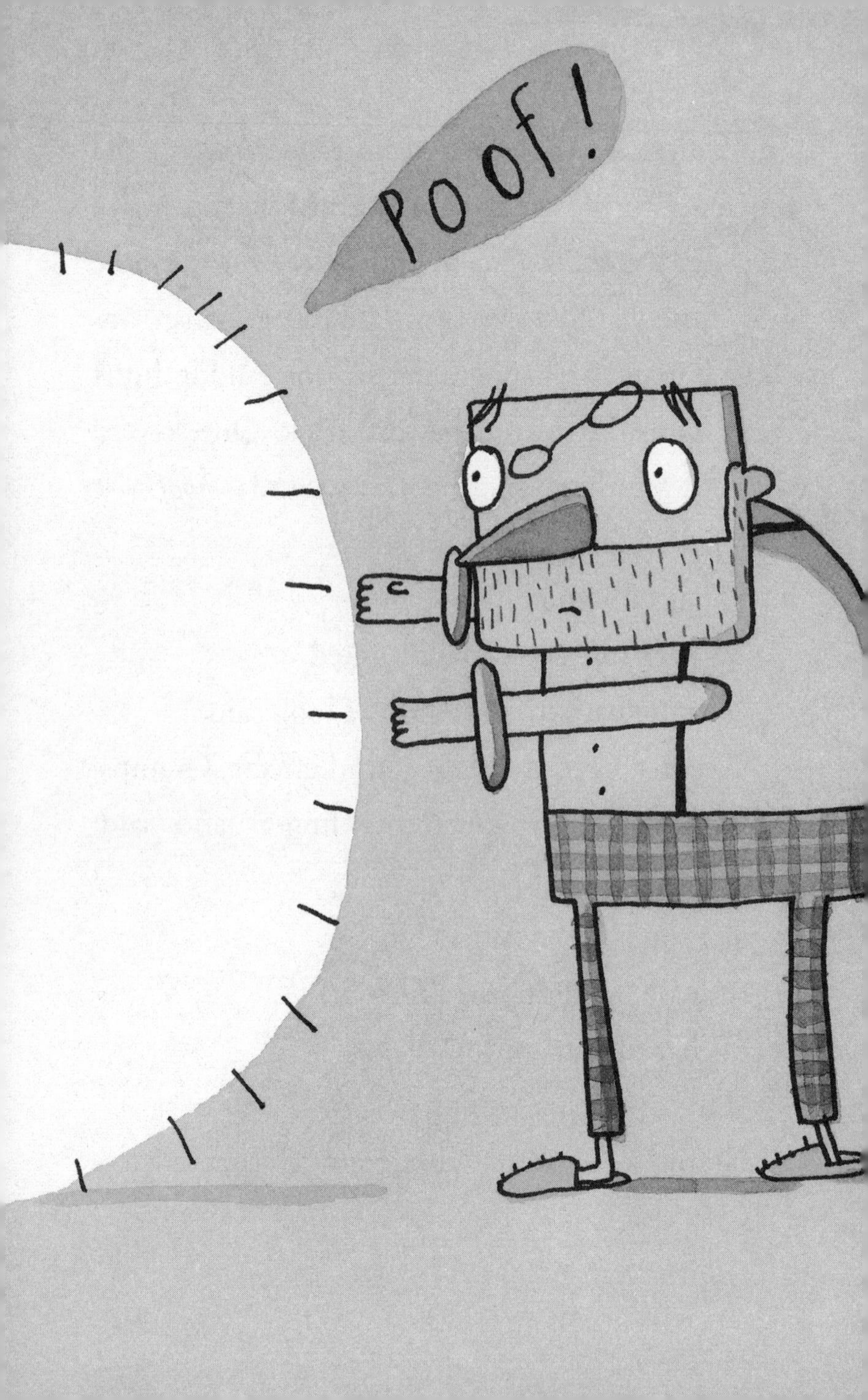
Poof!

his granddaughter had been standing. "I don't see you, Jo."

"You're not supposed to. That's why they call it invisibility," Jo said proudly, and if she had been visible, you could have seen her smiling from ear to ear. "It's all in the *poof,* Gramps."

Grandpa Joe got up from his chair. It wasn't every day your granddaughter turned invisible. He had to celebrate. Right in the middle of his little shack, he did the dance-of-the-retired-sheriff-whose-granddaughter-just-went-*poof!* Then he said, "Time to catch bad guys, Jo?"

Jo shook her invisible head. "Time to go to the movies."

7

Is This Seat Taken?

The movie was that one you've heard of. You know, with the handsome actor and the glamorous actress that involves a crime? That one.

Before heading to the movie theater, Jo unpoofed herself. She would be driving her Schmomobile, and if she did so while invisible, people would notice. This way it was just superhero Jo Schmo, speeding through the streets of San Francisco, probably in pursuit of some sort of villain.

Jo parked outside the theater, said, *"Poof!"* and

went inside. She found an empty seat and sat down. It was a great movie. Jo couldn't take her eyes off the handsome actor . . . Even the bad guys were cute.

But Jo was still invisible. The seat she occupied looked like it was *un*occupied. That's what the fat lady thought, anyway. She came late to the movie, looked at the seat where the invisible Jo Schmo was sitting, and said to herself, "I think I'll sit there."

So she did.

"*Squawk!*" went Jo.

"*Squawk!*" went the fat lady.

"Get off of me!" yelled Jo.

"Who said that?" said the fat lady. She tried to get comfortable. "Boy, this seat is lumpy."

And right in the middle of the squawking and the complaining about the lumpy seat, Jo's phone vibrated in her pocket—a text message from Grandpa Joe. Only Jo didn't realize it was a text message. She thought something bad was

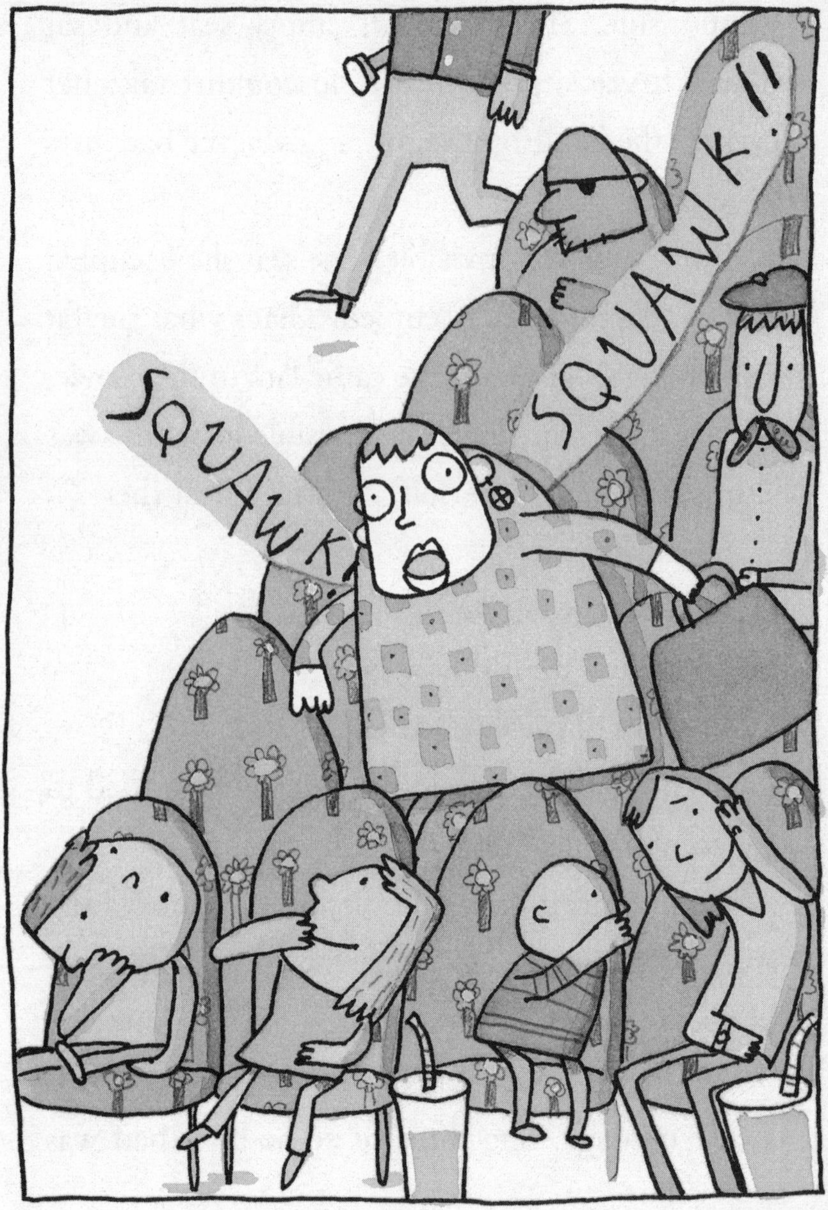
SQUAWK.
SQUAWK!!

happening to her leg because she was being squashed by a fat lady. This caused Jo to squawk even louder.

Finally, the lady decided to find a less lumpy seat (and one that didn't talk so much), and Jo ran out of the theater. Getting into the movies for free was not all it was cracked up to be.

Once outside, Jo unpoofed herself. Only then did she realize that her leg was vibrating not because it was about to fall off from being sat on by an enormous person, but because her grandfather had been trying to reach her.

And here's what he said:

Pirates are attacking a fashion show.
Go get 'em, Jo.

Jo sprinted across the parking lot to her Schmomobile, where the faithful Raymond was waiting. "Ready to catch bad guys, Raymond?"

Raymond gave her a look that said, "Is the sky blue? Do I like bacon? Is my jaw still sore from your Tasmanian Chop?"

Well, you get the idea.

"Sorry about the chop," Jo said as she hit the gas.

The fashion show was indeed a triple whammy. Lots of rich people to rob, plenty of grog to drink, and all sorts of pretty women to chase.

"I love triple whammies," Pinkbeard said to himself. He stood and watched as his crew of interesting fellows split up. Some of them went for the grog, some of them robbed the rich people, and some of them chased the beautiful fashion models.

Then they rotated. The pirates who had been robbing the rich people started chasing the fashion models, and the pirates who had been chasing the fashion models went after the grog.

The grog in question was wine, and Pinkbeard preferred lemonade. So right in the middle of the grog drinking, and the robbing of the rich people, and the chasing of fashion models, Pinkbeard wandered off in search of his drink of choice.

Lemonade. The pinker the better.

8

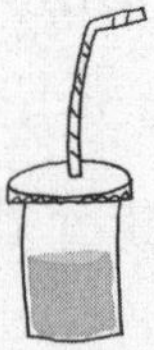

Revenge

Pinkbeard had no idea where to look for pink lemonade. He was hundreds of years in the future. Maybe they didn't make it anymore. Maybe they didn't even grow lemons. And now that he thought of it, why was pink lemonade pink? There was no such thing as a pink lemon.

The world was just a complicated place, Pinkbeard decided.

He wandered down Fisherman's Wharf and kept his eyes peeled for someplace where they might sell his favorite grog. He tried several bars, but none of them sold pink lemonade. Finally, Pinkbeard gave up and headed back to the fashion show to see how his crew was doing.

They were still equally divided between grog drinking, fashion-model chasing, and the robbing of rich people. Every now and then Bart would call out, "Rotate!" And the pirates who had been chasing fashion models would start robbing rich people, and the ones who had been drinking grog would start chasing fashion models.

Pinkbeard stood back and watched it all like a proud dad.

That is, until a little girl in a red cape arrived.

She had a dog with her who also wore a cape. And he drooled way more than any dog ever drooled in the long history of drooling. Pinkbeard couldn't believe his eyes. The little girl started tweaking the pirates' ears and twisting their toes until they cried out, "Ow, ow, ow," and "ow."

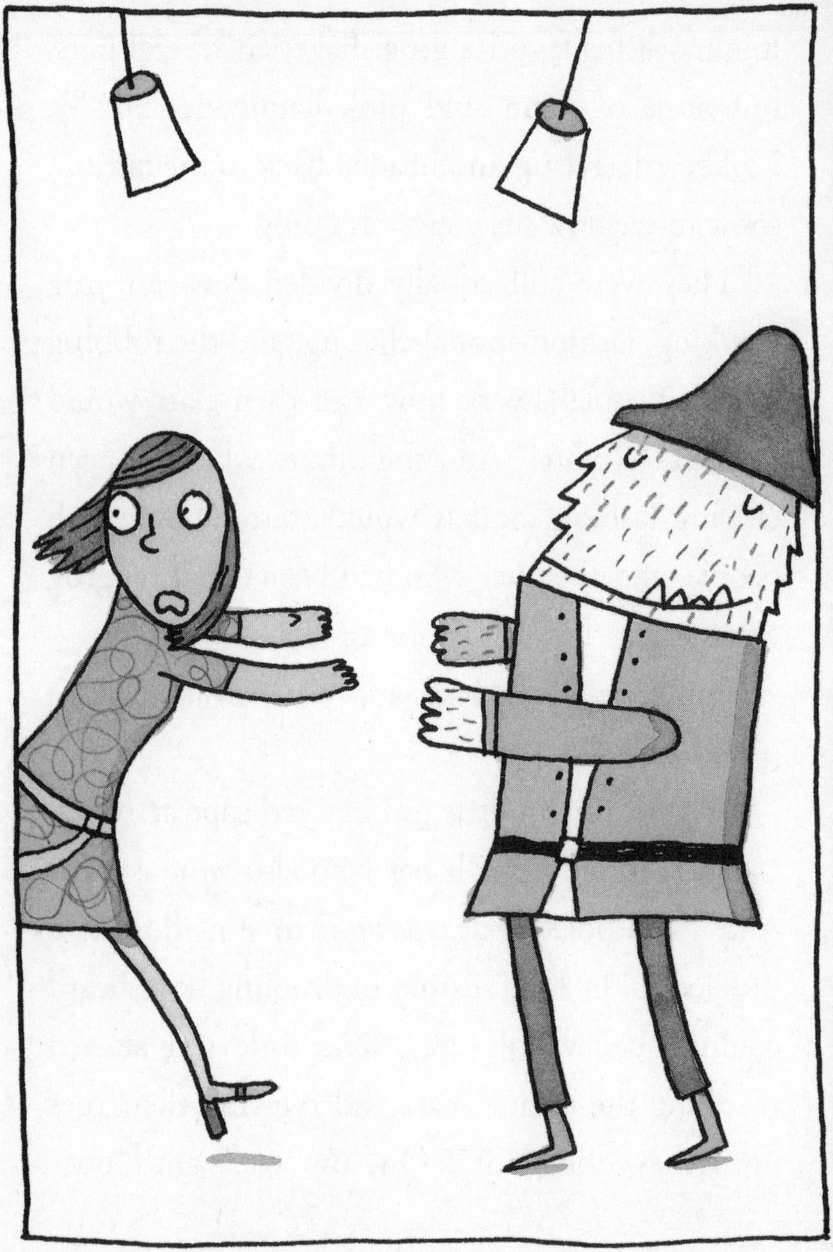

Some of them tried to run away, but they slipped on the dog drool.

The fashion models and the rich people cheered, "Hooray for Jo Schmo!"

"Jo Schmo," Pinkbeard said to himself. "Her name is Jo Schmo." He couldn't stand seeing his men getting their ears tweaked and their toes twisted. He was just about to jump in and help when the police showed up.

"Curse you, Jo Schmo," Pinkbeard muttered. "And your little dog, too." He usually didn't have anything against little girls, but this one with the cape was a different matter.

While the police started arresting his men, Pinkbeard slipped out the back. He'd have to find a way to rescue his men, but right now he had to run and hide. And maybe find some lemonade while he was at it.

Yes, that was it—find some pink lemonade and think things over.

Dr. Dastardly and Numb Skull were also in think-things-over mode. They had just escaped from prison, and now they wanted to get revenge on Jo Schmo and her slobbering sidekick.

"What's the plan, Dr. Dastardly?" Numb Skull asked. As you know, Numb Skull had spent way too many years getting knocked around inside the boxing ring to be any good at thinking, let alone

plotting revenge against a fourth grade superhero. He needed help. Fortunately, he was partners with a doctor.

And a dastardly doctor at that.

Only right now this dastardly doctor was all out of ideas. He had spent every ounce of his mental energy on exploding macaroni and an enormous slingshot.

"No plan?" Numb Skull asked.

"Not yet," Dr. Dastardly replied. "But we did escape from prison. That's a start. Let's go find something to drink and think things over."

And so the two of them wandered along Fisherman's Wharf in search of something to wet their whistles.

You would think that a couple of bad guys who just broke out of prison would find a bar or saloon to talk over their evil plan of revenge. Nope. These two went to a lemonade stand. Then they found a long bench and took a seat. At the end of this long bench sat a strange-looking guy with an eye patch and a pink beard.

"Now," said Numb Skull, "about Jo Schmo and her slobbering sidekick."

"Yes," said Dr. Dastardly. "Revenge is one of my favorite hobbies. I like it almost as much as taking over the world."

"You're my kind of guy. What's the plan, Dr. Dastardly?"

Dr. Dastardly and Numb Skull talked it over. And as they discussed their evil plan of revenge against Jo Schmo, the man with the pink beard at the end of the bench kept edging closer.

And closer . . .

Until he was practically on top of them.

"Do you mind?" said Dr. Dastardly to the man with the pink beard. "This is a serious discussion of revenge."

"I know," said the man with the pink beard. "Revenge against Jo Schmo. I would like to offer my assistance to your evil plan."

"You're my kind of guy," said Numb Skull.

Three Heads Are Better Than Two

Jo Schmo had no idea that one of the pirates had slipped away. After she got the best of them—all except one—she and Raymond jumped onto the Schmomobile and headed home. When they arrived, Jo went straight to the backyard and knocked on the door of her grandpa's shack.

"Who is it?" asked Grandpa Joe.

"It's Jo."

"Joe?"

"No, Jo."

"Oh, *Jo*. Come in, Jo. Thought I was talking to myself for a second there."

Jo opened the door and went in, leaving Raymond outside in case he decided to drool. Drooling to keep a bridge from blowing up was all fine and dandy. Drooling and making pirates fall down was also pretty cool. But drooling all over Grandpa Joe's shoes wasn't a pretty sight. In fact, it was kind of gross.

"How'd it go, Jo?" Grandpa Joe asked.

"The Russian Toe Hold worked perfectly. And you should have seen my Siberian Ear Tweak."

"What about the Tasmanian Chop?"

"I was so busy yanking ears and pulling toes that I forgot to use it."

"Maybe next time," Grandpa Joe said.

Jo nodded. Yes, next time she'd use nothing *but* the Tasmanian Chop. It was her newest move. If she didn't use it, she might forget how.

• • •

Across town, Dr. Dastardly and Numb Skull were getting to know their new partner and fellow revenge-seeker.

"If I didn't know better," Dr. Dastardly said, eyeing Pinkbeard's eye patch, "I'd say you are a pirate. Who are you?"

"Pinkbeard." Pinkbeard held up his glass of pink lemonade. "You are what you drink."

"I guess so," Numb Skull said. "How do you know Jo Schmo?"

"Ah," Pinkbeard began. "The lass captured my men, with the help of a very slobbery companion."

"Yes," Dr. Dastardly said, "he drools way more than any dog ever drooled."

"In the long history of drooling," added Numb Skull.

"Which is a very long history," said Pinkbeard. He should have known, since he'd been around for a couple of hundred years. And right then he told them his whole story. All about traveling forward in time from 17—, which is code for sometime that century.

"Whoa. Not only a pirate, but a time-traveling pirate." Dr. Dastardly was impressed. He held out his hand. "Mr. Pinkbeard, you're in the club."

"Your evil-bad-guy club?" Pinkbeard asked, shaking his hand.

"My get-back-at-Jo-Schmo club."

"That's my kind of club," Numb Skull said.

The problem was that Jo Schmo was a superhero with superpowers and super moves. Just by using her fingers, she could capture a band of pirates and make them say "Ow, ow, ow," and "ow."

They needed a super plan.

"Let's go have dinner and talk it over," Dr. Dastardly said. "Pink Lemonade is not enough."

Pinkbeard agreed that they would need a super plan to deal with Jo Schmo, and grog drinking was not enough.

But it was close.

10

Ask the Google

And so Dr. Dastardly, Numb Skull, and Pinkbeard went to a restaurant to talk seriously about getting back at Jo Schmo.

It was a pretty crowded restaurant. You would think that a pirate with a pink beard would be embarrassed to go out in public. Fortunately, there was a man at the bar with a blue beard, eating blueberries, and a guy eating a banana who had yellow hair.

Hold on a second. Only the banana *peel*

is yellow, so why would he have yellow hair? Hmm . . . go figure.

In any case, Pinkbeard fit right in. "You are what you eat," he said, gesturing to the men at the bar.

"I guess so," said Numb Skull.

They ordered their food and got down to business. "Okay," Dr. Dastardly began, "Jo Schmo is a superhero, and all superheroes have a weakness, right?"

Numb Skull nodded.

Pinkbeard said, "Arrrgh!" which is pirate talk for "What the heck are you talking about?" He continued, "Superhero? What's a superhero?"

Dr. Dastardly had forgotten that Pinkbeard was from a different century. How do you explain about superheroes to a person who has never heard of them?

Dr. Dastardly scratched his chin and thought it over. Then he looked across the table at Pinkbeard and said, "Ever hear of Achilles or Samson? Achilles had a weak heel, and when they cut Samson's hair, he lost his strength."

"Got it," said Pinkbeard. "The young lass has a weakness. What is it?"

"When in doubt, Google it," said Dr. Dastardly with a smile.

"Yes, Google it," Numb Skull agreed.

Pinkbeard looked confused. "What is this Google?" One of his men owned a *bugle*. But what the heck was a Google?

Life sure was complicated in the future.

Jo Schmo was pretty obsessed about turning invisible and getting into the movies for free. And doing so without getting sat on by a huge person. *I wonder if I would have enjoyed the movie if someone wasn't sitting on me,* she thought.

She didn't know. But that night, as she lay in bed, every time she closed her eyes, she saw the fat lady coming her way. Talk about a nightmare!

Nightmare or not, she had to try again. She had to go to the movies and not get squashed. She was pretty sure it could be done.

So after school the next day, she went to the movie theater and—

Poof!

Just like that, Jo Schmo was invisible. Then she went inside, found a seat, and scanned the room for large people.

"So far, so good," she said to herself. It was that

movie you've heard of. You know, the one with the handsome actor and the glamorous actress who are in love, only they don't realize it until the very end? That one.

It was pretty distracting to try to follow the movie while keeping an eye out for people who might sit on her. But she made it through without being squashed. She had no idea what the movie was about, but a least she didn't get sat upon.

Across town, a mad scientist, an ex-boxer, and a pirate with a pink beard entered the library. The librarian had green hair and was eating a green apple. Pinkbeard felt right at home.

"Show me this Google," Pinkbeard said. He wondered if it was anything like a bugle.

Dr. Dastardly walked up to a computer and typed *Jo Schmo's weaknesses* into Google. "Aha!" he said, which is code for "Looky here."

Numb Skull and Pinkbeard moved closer.

Dr. Dastardly stepped back and pointed to the screen. "Jo Schmo's weaknesses."

Superhero Jo Schmo's weaknesses are the three boys in her class at Prairie Street Elementary School—Kevin, Mitch, and David.

Kevin has the best hair.

Mitch looks spectacular in green.

David has exactly seventeen freckles, which Jo absolutely adores.

"That's it," said Dr. Dastardly. "We kidnap

Kevin, Mitch, and David, and when Jo comes to the rescue, she'll have no strength."

"Revenge City," said Numb Skull.

But Pinkbeard wasn't so sure. "What does Jo Schmo love? Go after what she loves. That's the pirates' way."

Dr. Dastardly gave Pinkbeard a confused look. "Huh?"

"I thought the pirates' way was to drink grog and chase women," said Numb Skull.

"That, too." Pinkbeard pointed to the computer screen. "What does Jo Schmo love?" he said again. "Ask the Google."

Dr. Dastardly typed it in. *What does Jo Schmo love?*

The answer came back with one word. *Raymond.*

Pinkbeard smiled. "The lass has a lad?"

"Nope," Numb Skull said. "Raymond's her dog."

The Eavesdropper

Former renowned newspaperman Jasper "Scoop" Johnson, who had given up journalism to write children's fantasy books, was having a rough time of it. No one wanted his stories. Not even the one about the giant gorilla who ate Milwaukee.

His mailbox was filling up with rejection letters, and Jasper was surprised to admit that he missed the newspaper business. He missed chasing down a new story. After all, his middle name was

Scoop. No one had a nose for a newspaper story like Jasper "Scoop" Johnson.

"If I can come up with the right story, I could get my old job back," Jasper said to himself as he browsed the children's book section of the library.

Yes, that was it, he decided. He just needed the right story.

And right there in the library, he found what he was looking for when he heard the word "Revenge."

Hearing the word gave Jasper tingles. There was a story nearby. He could feel it. He perked up his ears and peered over the bookcase, where he saw three suspicious villain types.

Former renowned newspaperman Jasper "Scoop" Johnson was trained to know suspicious villain types when he saw them. And these three looked very suspicious . . . and very villainy. One of them had a pink beard and an eye patch. Another one had a flattened nose, like he had been in way too many fights.

Jasper moved closer and listened in.

The guy with the pink beard was saying something about kidnapping a dog. The guy with the flat nose mentioned three names—Kevin, Mitch, and David.

The third guy threw his head back and laughed. *"Mwah-ha-ha!"* Right out loud. Right there in the library.

The green-haired librarian put a finger to his lips. "Shhhhhh!"

But the villain couldn't help himself. *"Mwah-ha-ha!"*

"An evil laugh," Jasper said to himself. Where you find an evil laugh, you find a story.

Jasper "Scoop" Johnson was back in business.

A few moments later, when Dr. Dastardly, Numb Skull, and Pinkbeard left the library, they had no idea they were being followed.

"What's the plan?" asked Numb Skull. He knew it had something to do with the three boys and Raymond, but he wanted more detail.

"We go after the dog first," Dr. Dastardly said. "Then we'll get the boys."

The problem was, how did you catch a superhero dog? Didn't they have super dog powers? They already knew that Raymond could drool more than any dog ever drooled in the long history of drooling. But did he bite harder than a normal dog? Could he run faster? Could he leap tall buildings in a single bound?

And more important, did he love what normal dogs loved?

"Like bacon," Pinkbeard said.

"And pork chops," Dr. Dastardly said.

"And pizza," Numb Skull added.

Pinkbeard had never heard of pizza. "I say we start with bacon."

"Bacon it is." Dr. Dastardly led the way back to his old hideout in the abandoned warehouse district. He pulled out a needle and thread and began to work on a human-size bacon costume. Actually, it was a Pinkbeard-size bacon costume.

But looking like a giant piece of bacon wasn't enough. To really get Raymond's attention, you had to smell like bacon. You might be thinking that smearing bacon all over yourself is pretty gross. You're not alone. Dr. Dastardly, Numb

Skull, and Pinkbeard thought so too. This did not stop the trio from breaking into a butcher shop late at night and grabbing all the bacon they could get their hands on. Then they smeared it all over Pinkbeard, who looked—and now smelled— exactly like a giant piece of bacon.

"I have to admit, you do smell delicious," Numb Skull said.

Pinkbeard had been called a lot of things over the course of his career—like marauder or pirate or someone-who-needs-a-bath. But this was the first time anyone had ever called him delicious. It had a certain ring to it.

The Bacon Dance

Jo Schmo was completely exhausted when she got home from the movie theater, where she had spent two full hours trying to watch a movie with one eye and look for people who might sit on her with the other. Try it sometime. It isn't easy.

She had no idea what the movie had been about . . . something about a romance, she thought, involving a handsome actor and glamorous actress.

Maybe it was best to use her invisibility powers to catch bad guys. This was what she thought as she flopped onto her bed. But the bad guys would have to wait. Jo Schmo couldn't keep her eyes open.

Before she drifted off, she tied a string around her big toe. The string led out the window and down to Grandpa Joe's shack. If anything happened in the middle of the night, Grandpa Joe would tug on the string and wake her up.

So Jo was sound asleep when a van pulled up in front of her house. Dr. Dastardly's van, that is. The one that had the sign painted on the side: DR. DASTARDLY, MAD SCIENTIST, FREE ESTIMATES.

And out of this van popped two evil bad guys and one gigantic piece of bacon.

"What do I do?" asked Pinkbeard.

"Go in the backyard and act delicious," said Dr. Dastardly.

How exactly does one behave in a delicious

manner? Pinkbeard wasn't sure. He went into the backyard, looked up at Jo's bedroom window, and did the Bacon Dance. This was a dance he made up on the spot . . . kind of like a hula dance with pork odor thrown in.

No dog could resist.

At least this was what Pinkbeard hoped.

Jo Schmo was snoring away, but not Raymond. He was wide awake, staring at the ceiling and counting sheep.

"Four hundred twenty-five," his look said. "Four hundred twenty-six . . ."

He stopped. Sheep-counting wasn't helping. Every time he pictured a sheep in his head, he wanted to chase it, and the thought of the chase was keeping him awake. Finally, he got to his feet and went to the window and looked out—

Raymond's mouth flopped open. He no longer

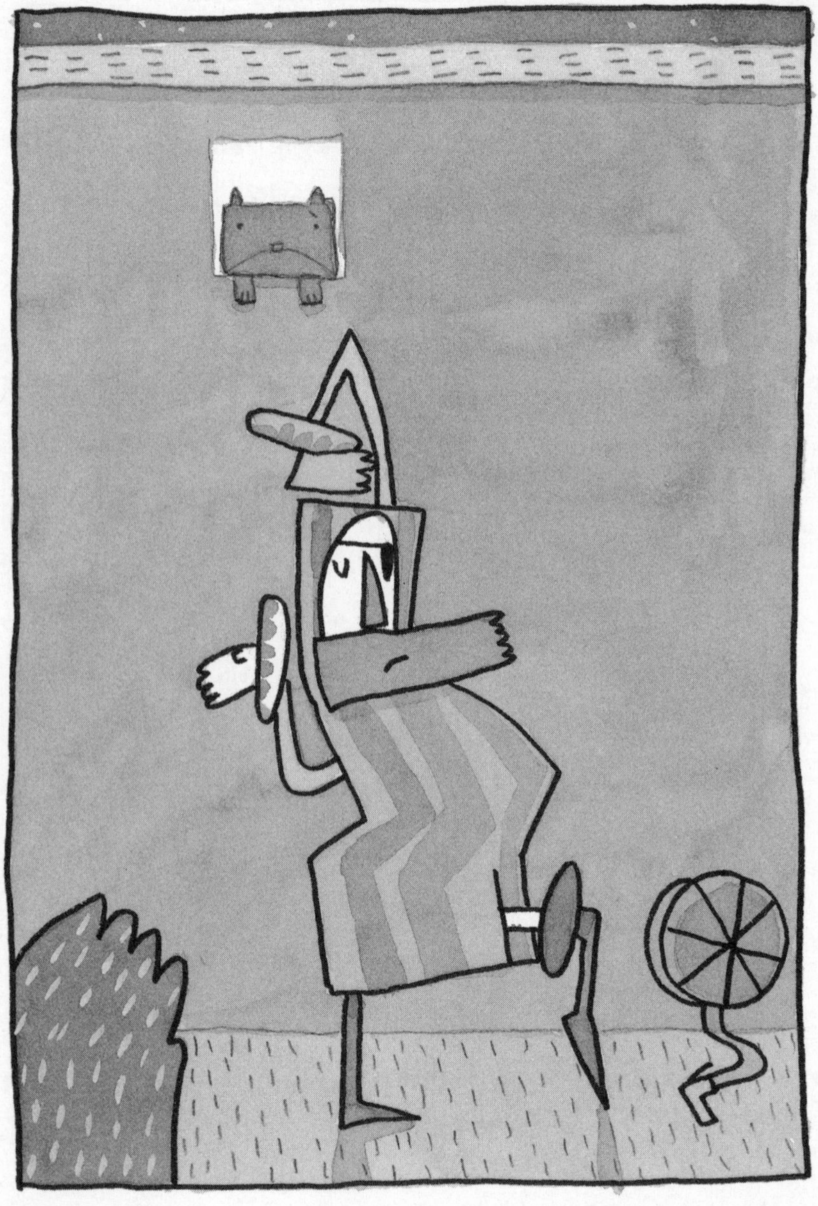

wanted to chase sheep. "Why chase sheep when there's a giant piece of bacon dancing in the moonlight in the backyard?" his look said.

This had to be some kind of dream. He rubbed his eyes with his paws and looked again. Nope, there was definitely an enormous piece of bacon dancing in the moonlight.

Raymond had never seen such a thing. He'd seen a giant sausage dancing in the moonlight, and a couple of times he'd seen dancing pork chops. But this dancing bacon was a first.

He ran outside to investigate. Boy, did that dancing bacon smell good. He moved closer for a better whiff . . . and possibly a nibble.

He never made it. Two figures jumped out of the bushes and grabbed him. One of them put a cloth to Raymond's nose. Raymond took one sniff, and everything went black.

"Chloroform," Dr. Dastardly said. "Works every time."

Dr. Dastardly and Numb Skull carried Raymond around to the front of the house and threw him into the van.

In a tree across the street sat former renowned newspaperman Jasper "Scoop" Johnson. You might think it would be difficult to jot down story notes while sitting on a tree branch. Well, if anyone could do it, Jasper "Scoop" Johnson could.

After the van pulled away, Jasper jumped to the ground. Then he climbed into his car and followed. There was more to this story than dognapping. He could feel it.

Raymond in Trouble

"Time for part two of our evil plan," Dr. Dastardly said as they raced through the city streets. He threw his head back. *"Mwah-ha-ha!"* The evil plan was working, and what better way to celebrate than with an evil laugh?

Pinkbeard climbed out of his bacon costume and said nothing.

"Don't pirates have evil laughs?" Dr. Dastardly asked. "I mean, what do you do when your evil plan is working? You have to celebrate somehow."

"True," said Pinkbeard.

"So what do you do?"

"I say, 'Drink up, me hearties, yo ho!'"

Dr. Dastardly nodded. "It's always about the grog with you pirates."

"Exactly," Pinkbeard said. "It's all about pink lemonade."

The trio drove across town to the abandoned warehouse district and dumped the unconscious Raymond into a huge room with concrete walls and an iron door. Even a superhero dog couldn't escape.

Yes, their evil plan was working.

"Mwah-ha-ha!" said Dr. Dastardly.

"Drink up, me hearties, yo ho!" Pinkbeard added.

Then they began work on part two of the plan: kidnapping the three boys from Jo Schmo's class, Kevin, Mitch, and David. Dr. Dastardly was pretty sure it would be easier to capture three fourth grade boys than it was to capture a superhero dog. At least no one would have to dress up like breakfast meat.

Too bad, Pinkbeard thought. He really liked doing the Bacon Dance.

When Raymond woke up, he found himself in a large room with concrete walls and an iron door. "Where am I?" his look said. The last thing he could remember was a gigantic piece of bacon dancing in the moonlight.

There was no sign of the bacon now. In fact, Raymond was completely alone. He went to the door and wiggled the knob. Locked.

Locked doors didn't worry Raymond. He was a superhero, or at least a superhero's sidekick. He had superpowers, didn't he? After all, he could drool more than any dog ever drooled in the long history of drooling. And that was a kind of superpower, wasn't it?

But did he have the strength to break through concrete walls and knock down iron doors? There was one way to find out.

Raymond threw himself against the iron door.

CRASH!

Not even a dent.

He ran full speed into the concrete wall.

SMACK!

Not even a scratch.

Nothing but a throbbing dog headache.

Raymond sat down, holding his head in his paws. "Not even a super dog could break through these walls," his look said.

He flopped to the ground . . . trapped. No way out. And right there, lying on the cold concrete floor, he vowed never again to mess with dancing bacon.

After a while, he rolled onto his back and looked up at the high ceiling. Moonlight was streaming

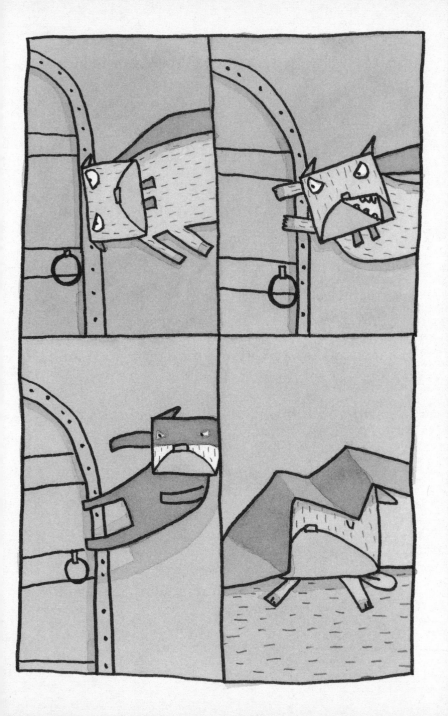

in. The walls were twenty feet high, but there was a window up there.

"If only . . ." Raymond's look said.

If only he could jump that high. Or even better, if only he could fly.

But wait . . . couldn't Jo Schmo fly? And wasn't he the sidekick? Raymond got to his feet and paced back and forth. Flying was all about thinking the right kind of lofty thoughts—that's what the *Superhero Instruction Manual* had said.

It was worth a try. "Lofty thoughts," Raymond's look said.

Truth, he thought, and leaped into the air.

CRASH! He hit the floor hard.

He tried again. *Justice.*

SMACK!

The American way.

PLOP!

He tried it with a running start. *All dogs are*

created equal, which is the loftiest thought he could come up with.

He jumped forward.

Then backward.

With his eyes closed.

On one leg.

On three legs.

But it was no use. No matter how hard he tried, Raymond couldn't get off the ground.

KABOOM!

You might be asking yourself, "What happened to the band of interesting fellows, otherwise known as Pinkbeard's band of pirates?" As you know, they were arrested after Jo Schmo stopped them from stealing from rich people and chasing fashion models. Not to mention drinking grog that didn't belong to them.

Drinking someone else's grog without permission is pretty sinister, if you think about it. And these guys were pirates. They drank straight from the bottle, and they didn't wipe it off. *Eew!*

So they were thrown in jail, and after a few days of waving angry fists in the air while saying things like, "Curse you, Jo Schmo, and your little dog, too!" the band of pirates got down to the business of making their escape.

They had heard that a mad scientist and an ex-boxer had just escaped from prison, using exploding macaroni and a giant slingshot.

"If only we knew how to blow up macaroni," said Bart, who was now the leader.

But try as he might, he couldn't find a way to make macaroni explode.

So he made chocolate pudding explode instead. *KABOOM!*

Imagine brown goo flying in every direction. It's kind of . . . disgusting.

The guards thought so too. So did the other inmates. And while the guards and the other inmates were being disgusted and wiping brown

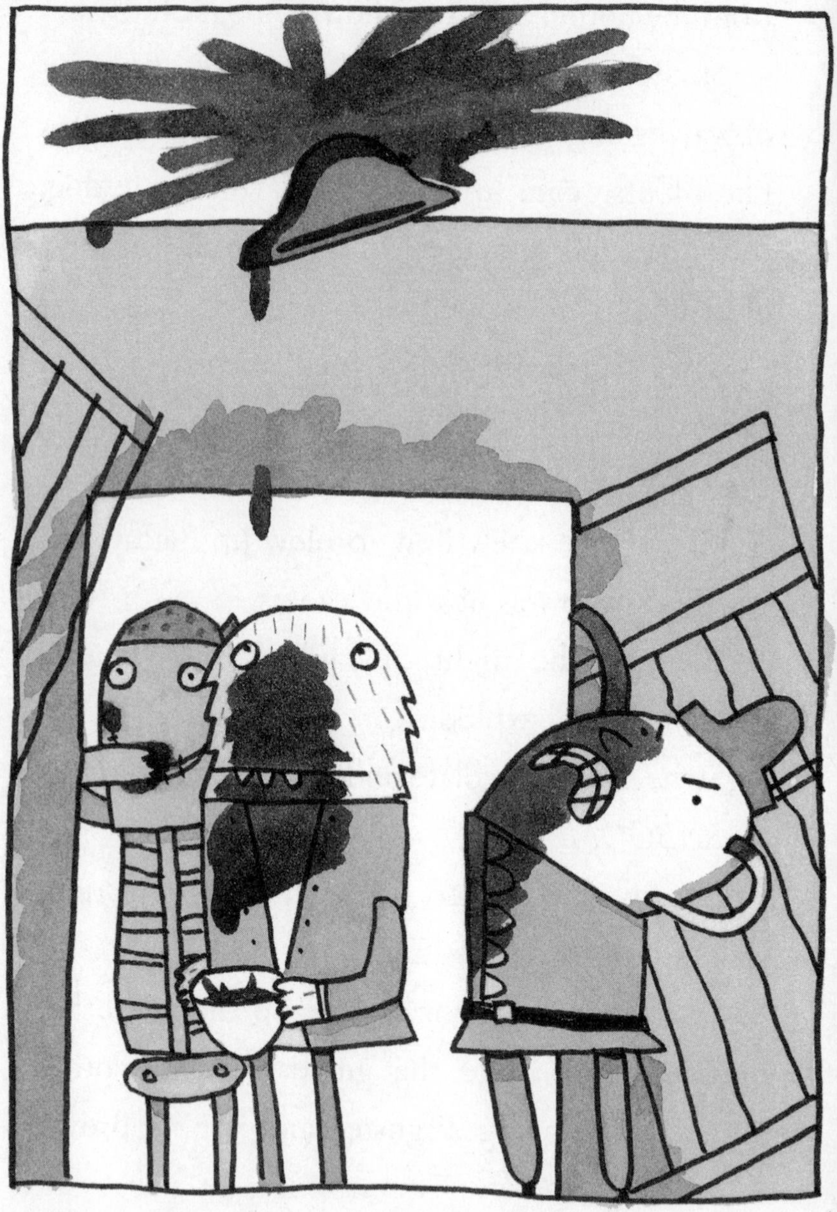

goo out of their eyes, Bart and the rest of the pirates disguised themselves as guards and walked right out the front door of the jail.

"Free at last!" said Bart with a smile. Then he turned to his men. "Drink up, me hearties, yo ho!"

They would be happy to drink up, if they could find some grog.

"Back to the ship," Bart suggested. Pirate ships were loaded with grog.

Pinkbeard had no idea that his fellow pirates had escaped from jail and were now back on the ship, drinking grog. He was too busy working on part two of their evil plan: kidnapping the three boys, Kevin, Mitch, and David.

They went after Kevin first, snatching him right from his bed.

"He does have a great head of hair," Numb Skull observed.

They tied him up and threw him into the van.

Then they drove over to Mitch's house and yanked him right out of his bedroom window. Mitch was wearing his green pajamas, and everyone agreed that he did look rather spectacular.

David was the last boy to be kidnapped. It was too dark to see his freckles, but they were as adorable as usual. Trust me.

"Revenge time," Dr. Dastardly said as he hit the gas and they sped back to the abandoned warehouse district. The Bad Doctor couldn't help smiling. It was, after all, the perfect crime. They had what Jo Schmo loved and they had her weakness. "When she shows up to rescue the dog, she'll no longer be Jo Schmo, Superhero. She'll be just plain Jo Schmo."

"Revenge time," Numb Skull said.

"Revenge time," Pinkbeard agreed. "Drink up, me hearties, yo ho!"

They'd drink up later. Revenge time came first.

Jasper "Scoop" Johnson

Jasper "Scoop" Johnson was sitting on another tree branch, jotting down story notes—all about a trio of bad guys who had kidnapped three boys and a dog. But the more he wrote, the more he realized he couldn't just tell the story. He had to do something about it.

He had to tell Jo Schmo.

Plus, his rear end was getting a little sore from writing a story while sitting on a tree branch. He needed a break. So he jumped out of the tree, got in his car, and raced across town to Jo Schmo's house.

In the backyard he came across the string that led from Jo's bedroom window to her grandfather's shack. He grabbed the string and *tugged, tugged, tugged.* When nothing happened, he did it again. *Tug, tug, tug.*

Jo Schmo was fast asleep, dreaming of grog-drinking, fashion-model-chasing pirates. Not to mention the sort of pirate who robbed rich people. She was also dreaming of a fat lady sitting on her.

Talk about a nightmare.

While the fat lady was trying to sit on Jo, the pirates were tugging on her toe. *Tug, tug, tug.* They were not only pirates—they were also experts in the Russian Toe Hold. *Tug, tug, tug.*

Jo sat up in bed, opened her eyes, and saw the string tied to her big toe *tug-tug-tugging.* It wasn't the Russian Toe Hold after all.

Tug, tug, tug.

"Wake up, Raymond," she said, jumping to her feet. "Grandpa Joe needs us."

Raymond, who always slept at the foot of her bed, was not there.

"Raymond?" Jo said again.

Grandpa Joe was supposed to be listening to his police radio, waiting for news of any crimes being committed so he could alert his granddaughter about them. But he had drifted off to sleep. Before doing so, he had tied the string around his big toe.

Now he was snoring away, dreaming of doing battle with bad guys of every shape and size. Grandpa Joe was a retired sheriff, and this is what sheriffs dream about: fighting crime, doing battle with bank robbers, drug dealers, gang members, and—

Experts in the Russian Toe Hold?

Tug, tug, tug. Tug, tug, tug.

He opened his eyes and saw that it was the string attached to his toe doing the tugging. He untied it and ran outside.

Jo Schmo was already there.

"What is it, Jo?" he asked.

"What is it, Gramps?" Jo said.

And that's when they noticed that they were not alone. Jasper "Scoop" Johnson was standing there, still holding the string.

"What's the meaning of this?" Grandpa Joe asked.

"Your dog has been kidnapped," Jasper said.

"Raymond?"

Jasper nodded.

"Who?" asked Jo. "Where?" She also wanted to know why and how, but who and where were good enough for starters.

Jasper told them as much of the story as he knew, all about the dancing bacon, the chloroform, the getaway vehicle, and what was painted on the side—DR. DASTARDLY, MAD SCIENTIST, FREE ESTIMATES.

"There were three of them," Jasper said, "if you count the bacon."

Dr. Dastardly and Numb Skull, Jo thought. She had heard about their prison break. *But who was the third member of the evil trio?* Jo had no idea, and she couldn't waste any more time trying to figure it out. Raymond was in trouble.

She fired up the Schmomobile and was about to hit the gas when Jasper said, "They also kidnapped three boys."

"Wow," Grandpa Joe said, "that's some pretty ambitious bacon." Then he turned to his granddaughter. "Go get 'em, Jo!"

16

"Yoo-Hoo!"

If you were walking along in the abandoned warehouse district, and you wandered past a concrete building with an iron door, you might hear things like *Pow, Crash, Thud, Plop* . . . and now and then *SPROINK!*

If you were inside the concrete building with the iron door, you'd see a dog with a look on his face that said, "Ouch," and "I am one miserable mutt."

This would be Raymond. And he really was one miserable mutt. He had tried hundreds of times to get up in the air while thinking lofty thoughts. Not only thoughts like *Truth, Justice,* and *All dogs are created equal,* but other lofty thoughts, such as *Kindness* and *Forgiveness* and *Don't drink out of the toilet.*

But none of it worked, and Raymond was getting tired of crashing to the floor.

"If only I had stayed away from that bacon," his look said.

Of course, he couldn't have. Bacon was his favorite, and a giant piece of it dancing in the moonlight was irresistible . . . and rather yummy.

"That's it!" Raymond's look said as he got to his feet. "Bacon is the loftiest thought of all!"

Bacon, he thought, and leaped into the air.

This time he didn't crash to the floor. He kept going up.

Bacon, he thought again, and he went a little higher.

Bacon. He rose higher still.

And before you could say "Raymond flew to the top of the room and crashed through the window," Raymond flew to the top of the room and crashed through the window.

"Free at last!" his look said. He flew above the abandoned warehouse district and out over the bay. He dove toward the water. Then he rose up again, getting the hang of his new superpower. He zigged and zagged. He sped up and slowed way down until he was almost hovering in place.

Finally, he started for home. "Jo Schmo has got to see this," Raymond's look said, and he headed back to Crimshaw Avenue.

Jo Schmo would have been proud of her flying sidekick, but she wasn't home. She was racing through the streets of the abandoned warehouse district, searching for him.

How do I find Raymond? Jo asked herself. The answer was easy: Where you find large amounts of drool, you find Raymond. After all, he drooled way more than any dog ever drooled in the long history of drooling.

Jo looked around, heading down one street after another, looking for something wet and drool-like shimmering in the moonlight. So far nothing but dry pavement.

And then—

There it was. Something was seeping out from beneath an iron door on a concrete building.

"Drool," Jo said out loud as she pulled to a stop. "Raymond, are you in there?"

No answer.

High above the door, there was a broken window. "Sponge cake," Jo said. This was the lofty thought that caused her to get off the ground. She flew to the top of the building and in through the broken window. But there was no dog in sight.

Drool everywhere, but no Raymond.

Dr. Dastardly was in his lair, along with Numb Skull, Pinkbeard, and three of Jo's classmates. Kevin, Mitch, and David were bound and gagged, but you could still see that Kevin had great hair, Mitch looked spectacular in his green pajamas, and now in the light, David's freckles clearly were as adorable as ever.

The lair was next to the concrete building where the villains had been keeping Raymond. They didn't know that the dog had escaped, but now they could hear Jo calling for him.

Dr. Dastardly opened the door and stuck his head out. "Yoo-hoo! Jo Schmo!"

By now Jo was on the street again. "Where's my dog?" she said. "What have you done with him, Dr. Dastardly?"

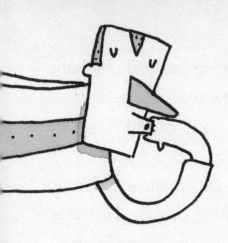

"Come in and see for yourself," he replied.

You might be thinking that Jo should have smelled a trap. After all, this was Dr. Dastardly she was dealing with. But Jo was too worried about Raymond to think much of anything. Plus, it was the middle of the night, and her brain was still half asleep.

Too bad.

Jo Schmo went inside and came face to face with not her favorite pet, but her three weaknesses, Kevin, Mitch, and David.

She fell to her knees and let out a feeble, "Yikes!"

"Now what?" asked Numb Skull.

Dr. Dastardly didn't say anything. He had Jo Schmo in his clutches, but what should he do next? He was a mad scientist, not an expert in revenge.

"Amateurs," Pinkbeard said. "Follow me. I know exactly what to do with her."

17

"Arrrgh!"

Dr. Dastardly glanced over at Pinkbeard. "You know what to do? Really?"

"I'm a pirate," Pinkbeard said. "I do this kind of thing for a living."

"So what's the plan?" Dr. Dastardly felt a little strange asking someone else what the plan was. He was used to other people asking *him* what the plan was. Still, if Pinkbeard had one, Dr. Dastardly was all ears.

"Grab the girl and the boys and follow me," Pinkbeard said.

"Where to?" asked Numb Skull.

"Back to my ship," the pirate commanded.

Dr. Dastardly crossed his arms. "And the plan is?"

"We'll have the lass walk the plank."

"Good plan."

When they got to Pinkbeard's ship, they saw all the other pirates drinking grog and celebrating their escape from jail.

"Nice work," Pinkbeard said to Bart. Then he turned to his men and began barking out commands. Soon the ship was heading into the deep waters of the bay.

Jo Schmo, whose feet and hands were now bound tight, could do nothing. As long as Kevin, Mitch, and David were near, Jo was just an ordinary fourth grade girl with no superpowers at all.

"Sorry, guys," she said. "I'm all out of strength today."

Bart tied a blindfold over Jo's eyes and shoved her out onto the plank. Then he poked her with the end of his sword. "Keep moving, sister."

Jo inched forward along the plank while Dr. Dastardly, Numb Skull, and Pinkbeard looked on.

"Revenge time," said Pinkbeard. He almost added, "Drink up, me hearties, yo ho!" but he had to wait for Jo to hit the water. Then he'd celebrate.

Bart gave Jo another poke with his sword as she stood at the very end of the plank. "One more step, please."

Jo heard the splash of the black waters of the bay. She felt the tip of the sword in her back. And then—

"Look, up in the sky!"

"It's a bird."

"It's a plane."

"No, it's that slobbering sidekick."

Yes, it was the slobbering sidekick. Raymond swooped out of the sky like a crop-dusting plane and laid down a patch of drool on the deck of the ship. Then he doubled back and did it again. Pirates started slipping all over the place. It was like a hockey match. One pirate slammed into another pirate, who slammed into another. Some fell overboard.

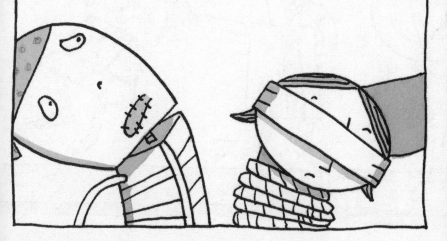

Pinkbeard pulled out his pistol and fired. But Raymond was too quick for him.

"Arrrgh!" yelled Pinkbeard, which is code for "Stay still so I can shoot you."

But Raymond did not stay still. He was too busy laying down drool all over the ship. Even on the . . . uh . . . poop deck.

Jo Schmo was blindfolded and couldn't see a thing. But she heard it. Did someone mention

Raymond? Had he come to her rescue? In the middle of the bay?

Jo had to find a way to help. She took a step.

Unfortunately, it was a step in the wrong direction. She fell from the plank into the freezing waters of the bay, and down she went.

Glub, glub.

Glub, Glub

Jasper "Scoop" Johnson didn't get his job back, even though he had written a great story about a trio of bad guys and a quadruple kidnapping. But Jasper didn't care. He really liked going into Jo's backyard and pulling on that string. He liked helping a superhero.

And now as he sped across the bay on his Jet Ski toward a pirate ship, he said, "Maybe Jo Schmo could use another sidekick."

Catching bad guys for a living sounded like way more fun than *writing* about them.

"That's strange," he said as he neared the pirate ship. "It looks like they're having a hockey match on deck."

Jasper watched as pirate slammed against pirate. Some fell overboard.

And then he spotted Jo Schmo. But she wasn't the superhero he'd written about. This looked like an ordinary girl, tied up, standing on the end of a plank.

Suddenly, this ordinary girl plunged into the bay.

Jasper pulled back hard on the throttle, and the Jet Ski picked up speed. He skipped over the waves. When he reached the pirate ship, he hit the brakes.

Jet Skis don't have brakes, but you get the idea.

Jasper dove after Jo Schmo. Luckily, he had on

his glow-in-the-dark wetsuit. It gave off just enough light so he could see what he was doing. And what he was doing was saving a tied-up superhero.

As Jo Schmo sank into the freezing waters of the bay, she got farther and farther away from the ship and farther and farther from Kevin, Mitch, and David. And the farther she got from her weaknesses, the stronger she felt.

Strong enough to break the ropes.

Only breaking the ropes wasn't enough. Jo couldn't swim.

A superhero who doesn't know how to swim? I know . . . Go figure.

Jo kicked her arms and legs, but it didn't help. She continued to sink . . . and worse, a glowing sea creature was coming at her from above.

This is a very bad day, Jo thought. *Drowning is bad enough. Now I'm going to be eaten by a glow-in-the-dark sea monster.*

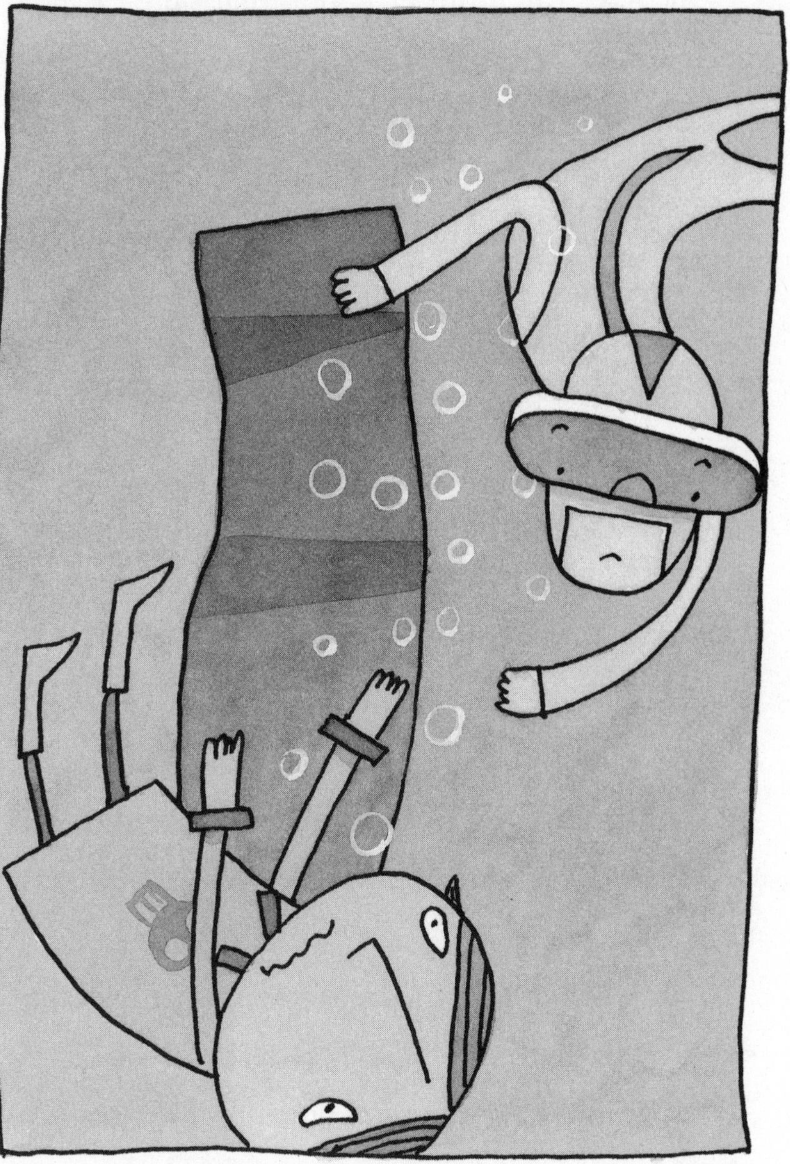

She gave the monster a look that said, "Please don't eat me."

Jasper "Scoop" Johnson was not a glow-in-the-dark sea monster. He wasn't a sea monster at all. He was a former renowned newspaperman and former aspiring children's book writer who was now trying to become a superhero's sidekick.

He had to rescue Jo Schmo for that to happen.

As he swam deeper, he saw Jo give him a look that said, "Please don't eat me."

Please don't eat her? He wouldn't think of such a thing.

Jasper grabbed Jo by the cape. Then he opened his mouth to tell her that he didn't eat superheroes—besides, he was a vegetarian. He was there to rescue her.

But when he opened his mouth to explain, seawater poured in. Lots of seawater.

Jasper and Jo sank to the bottom of the bay.

Jo Gretzky

Jo Schmo was relieved that it was just someone in a glow-in-the-dark wetsuit, not a sea monster with an appetite. She gave him a look that said, "We're underwater—try not to speak."

Too late. Jasper tried to give her a look that said something, but he was too busy drowning.

And that's when someone grabbed him from above. Jasper, who was still holding on to Jo Schmo's cape, felt himself being dragged toward the surface.

And just in time, too.

Seconds later, Jasper and Jo broke the surface and gulped a breath of fresh air. Make that three breaths of fresh air. Then they looked over at their mystery rescuer.

It was Raymond, who was giving them a look that said, "Ta-da!"

"Get the boys, Raymond," Jo said.

Bacon, Raymond thought. He flew up to the deck of the ship, grabbed Kevin by the collar, and took off with him.

Jasper climbed up the anchor chain and untied Mitch and David. Then the three of them climbed down to Jasper's Jet Ski.

As the boys raced away from the ship, Jo's full superhero strength returned.

"Sponge cake!" she yelled, and she rose out of the water. She flew up to the deck of the ship and joined in the hockey match, skating over the slobber like Wayne Gretzky. She body-checked a few of the pirates over the side, even the ones on the . . . uh . . . poop deck.

Bart came at her with his sword, but Jo was too quick for him.

CHOP! The Tasmanian Chop worked perfectly.

Then she went after Numb Skull.

CHOP!

Dr. Dastardly.

CHOP!

And Pinkbeard.

CHOP!

By this time Raymond, who had dropped Kevin off on the Golden Gate Bridge, had come back to help. Raymond wasn't the best hockey player in the world . . . but he wasn't bad.

More pirates came at them.

CHOP! CHOP!

When the chopfest was complete, Jo got busy tying up the trio of bad guys, along with the others. Raymond tried to help, but he didn't have hands.

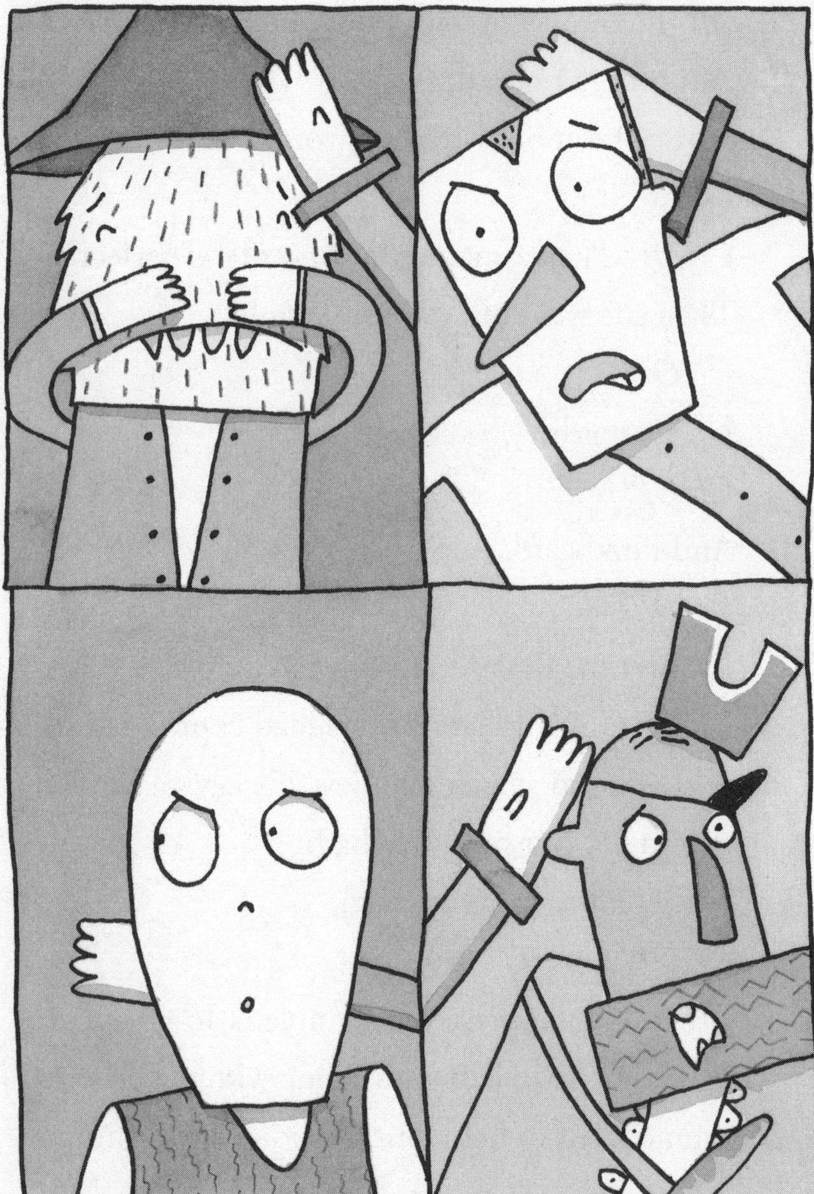

Word got around that a rowdy hockey match was happening on a pirate ship in the middle of the bay. The Coast Guard cruised by to investigate. It was a hockey match, all right. They could see a girl in a red cape, skating around like Wayne Gretzky, bumping into people.

Not just people . . . pirate people.

"You're under arrest," the captain of the Coast Guard called out. He really wanted to watch the hockey match. But he knew pirates when he saw them. He also recognized Jo Schmo.

"Thanks, Jo. We'll take it from here."

Jo nodded. "Sponge cake," she said, and up she went.

Bacon, Raymond thought, and joined her.

Together they flew across the bay, heading back to Crimshaw Avenue. Jo glanced over at her dog with new admiration. He'd survived being kidnapped by a giant piece of bacon, he'd saved her life . . . and now here he was flying beside her.

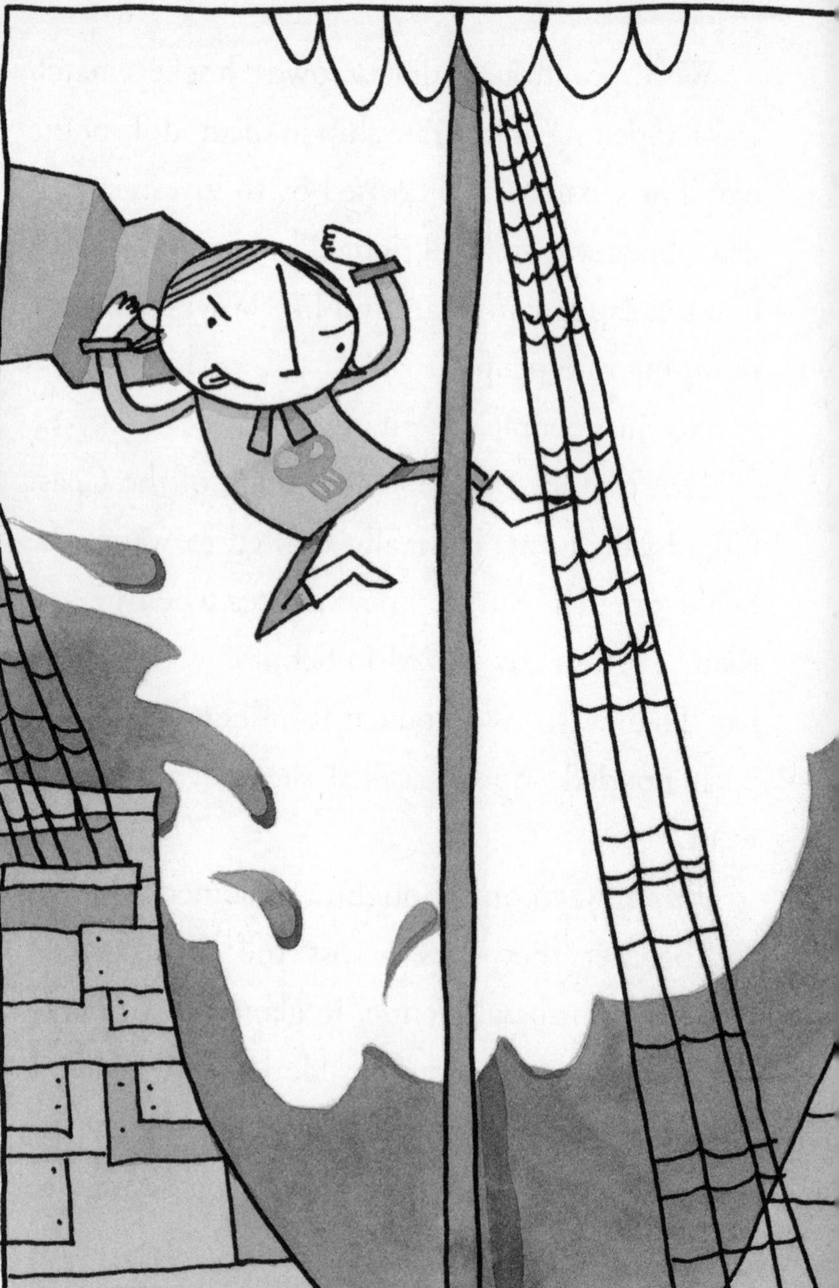

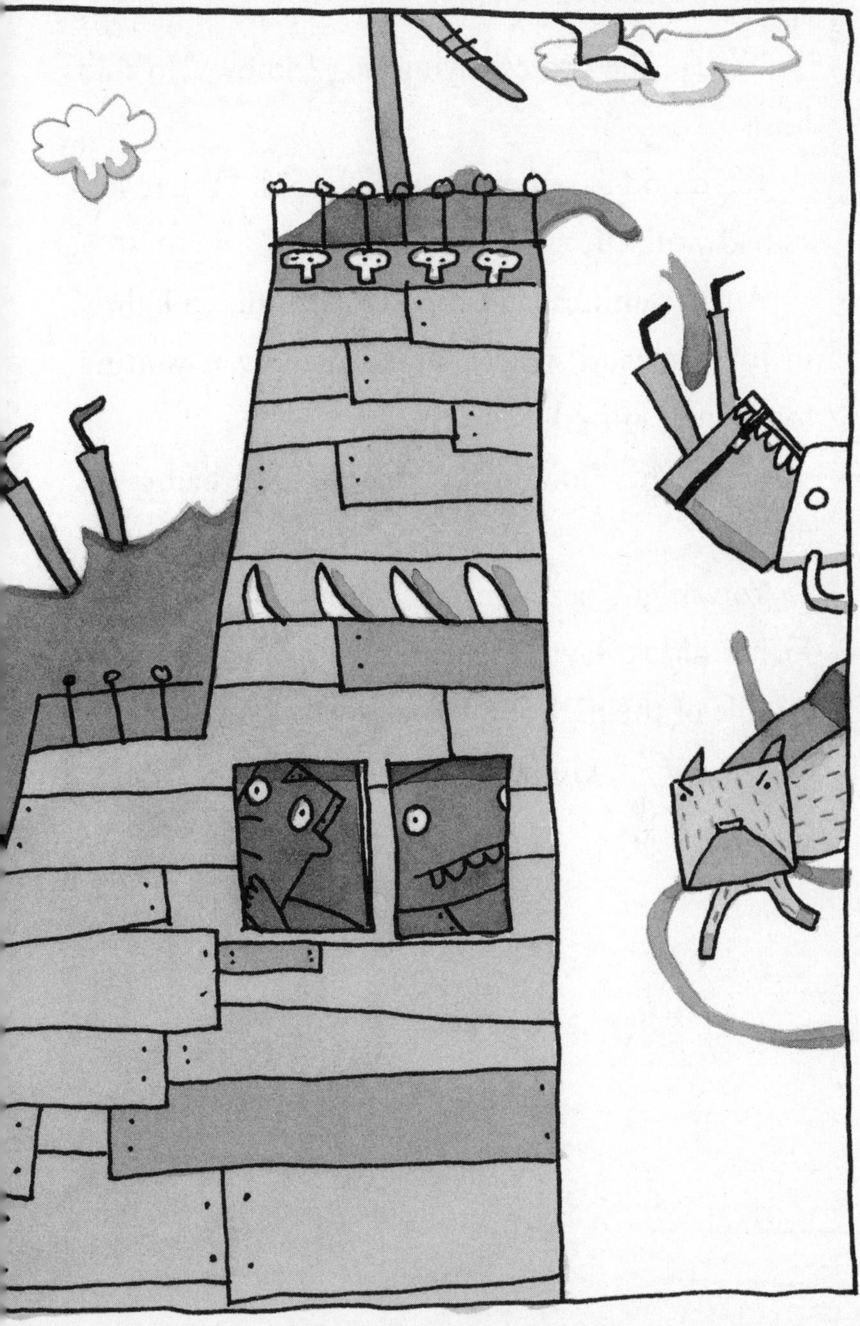

"You're the coolest flying dog I know," Jo told him.

Raymond gave her a look that said, "You're not so bad yourself."

A few minutes later they touched down lightly in Jo's backyard, where Grandpa Joe was waiting for them. "How'd it go?" he asked.

Jo smiled. "Jo and Raymond, eight; bad guys, nothing."

You might be saying to yourself, "Hooray for Jo, but didn't Raymond leave Kevin all alone in the middle of the night on the Golden Gate Bridge?"

I know . . . Go figure.

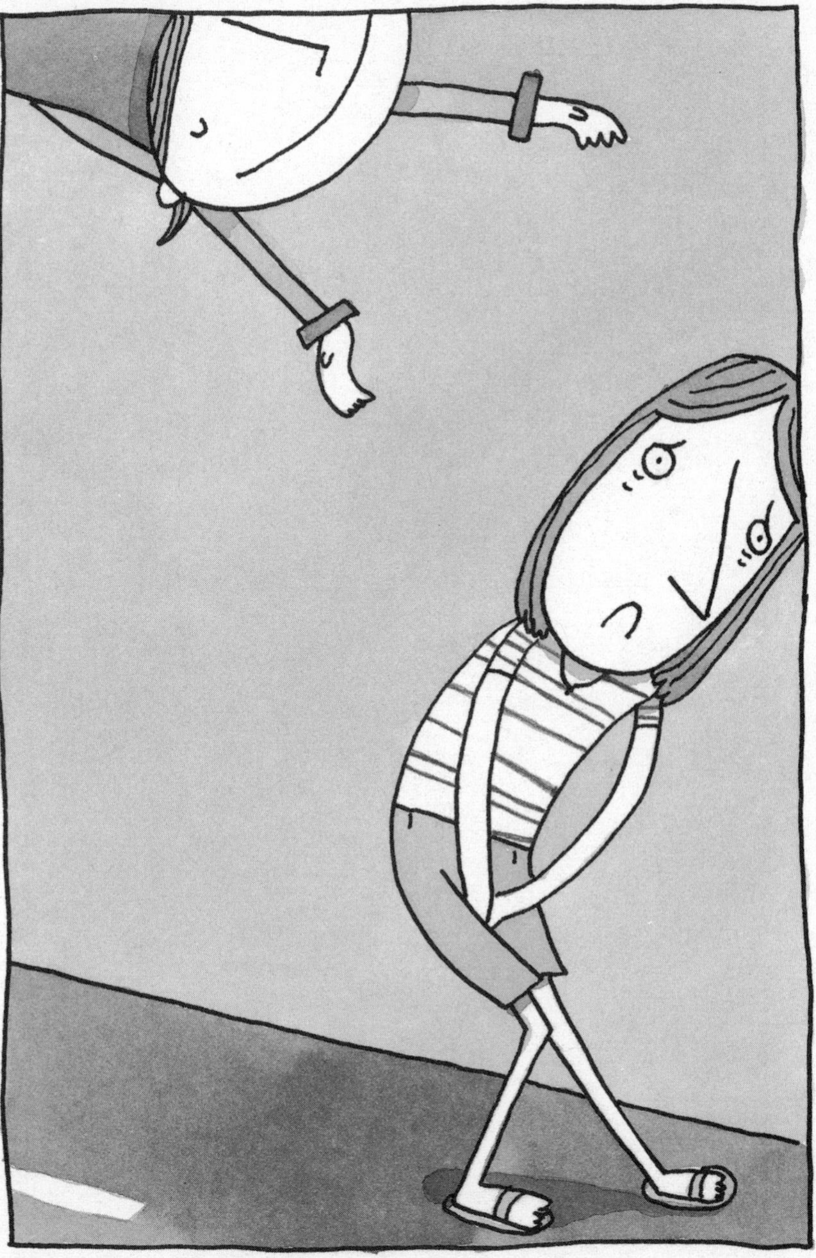